WHAT KIND OF DAY

SIX 32 CENTRAL #1

MINA V. ESGUERRA

BRIGHT GIRL BOOKS

MAP OF METRO MANILA

1

M akati, 7:45 a.m.

THE GUY WAS DEFINITELY NOT part of her tour group, and he knew it, too. He knew it, she knew it, and still after they locked eyes for maybe ten seconds of mutual knowing, he pulled the handle of the van's sliding door and let himself inside.

What the hell? Naya Llamas counted her breaths and wondered what to do, given this new situation. Six people were officially part of her tour today. She had rented a van that would comfortably fit ten. An extra person wouldn't push anyone out, but the unexpectedness wasn't cool. It was already going to be a long day.

This was not how she did things.

The designated meetup time at the park-adjacent parking lot was eight a.m., and she told the group they'd be leaving promptly at eight-ten. She had a reputation for being serious about time, and her guests today would know that. She would have to settle this *problem* in a few minutes, or else it would show up in a review somewhere that...that she had a stowaway? That she couldn't deal with one? What was this, even?

Only six people on this tour but if the situation got out of control, no telling how bad it could get. Naya's "income-generating hobby" relied on referrals from happy guests, and she needed to make this *hobby* last with every fiber of her being.

In a second, she was in the van to confront the guy.

He took a window seat on the last row, and was already tuning out the world. Earphones on, blank stare activated. Handsome face, sure, dark hair, growing stubble, and the look of someone who needed sleep and peace of mind.

None of that mattered! Her van, her tour, her rules.

"Excuse me," Naya said, tapping the seat directly in front of him, then the window near his face because the first tap didn't work. "Sir."

He pulled one earbud off. "Yeah?"

Yeah? He was just going to *yeah* his way out of this? The nerve. "This van is for a tour that starts at eight-ten a.m."

"Awesome."

"You are not part of the tour group."

"Oh. Yes, yes in fact I'm not."

"If you're not part of the tour, I'm going to have to ask you to—"

"I'd like to join it."

"It's not—" *It's not possible*, was what she was ready to say. Stubborn since birth. Resisting reasonable authority. Naya was aware of her flaws—other people made sure she knew them, all her life—but starting the "income-generating hobby" got her acquainted with a new side of her. More mature, more responsible. She also needed money to live. *Still.* "I have a website and a schedule and a waiver that you didn't—"

"How much is the tour?"

Damn, how far was he going to take this? She told him. And when she did, with that confident tone she practiced because she told herself to be proud of her value, she saw that he did not expect it to cost that much. Naya's tours were special, designed for specific experiences that she got to determine. Customizing the stops and setting the price high also kept a lot of the creeps and troublemakers away, so this could probably solve her problem before the van warmed up, and her long day could proceed as planned.

But in response, the guy fished his wallet from the pocket of his jeans, and opened it up. Worn and creased leather, thick with *stuff.* He dug in there and slowly extricated one bill after another. Eventually he had enough thousands to cover exactly what she said the tour cost.

"It's not that simple," she sputtered. "There's a waiver..."

"Your phone," he said. "Take a video of me."

"What?"

"Hold up your phone now, to my face. Take video."

She frowned, set the cash down on the seat, and did as he asked.

"Game? Okay. My name is Benjamin Cacho, of legal age, and I am joining this tour group of my own free will and you...what's your name?"

"Naya Llamas."

"...Naya Llamas, you are not liable for anything that happens to me while I'm on your tour today." He paused, and sort of shook his head. "In fact, any pain that befalls me today will be entirely my fault, I am sure. You can end the video now."

She did. "You don't even know where we're going, Benjamin Cacho."

"Today I just want to be anywhere but where I usually am. Anything else I need to do to join your tour, Naya Llamas?"

No, nothing else. More than anything, she wanted to throw the cash back at him, all dramatic like that, and tell him to go to the website and get on the waiting list like everyone else. People paid good money to get a spot on her tours and this display of casual disregard for what it was and what he had walked into was *disrespectful, damn it.*

But she needed the money. It was an objective reality, that most people in her life validated. *You are thirty-one. We shouldn't have to worry about you anymore,* her family members liked to say, or at least hint heavily.

"Say please," she said.

"Please." He let that go so quickly. He obviously did not have the same deadly sin as hers as a potential downfall.

"All right," she said. "And you can call me Naya."

"I'm Ben. And if my presence makes you uncomfortable, you don't need to call me anything. I will be quiet as a mouse."

"I don't like mice."

"I will be as quiet as your favorite quiet thing."

Naya sighed and picked up the money on the seat. No more reasons to resist; she put up enough of a fight, didn't she? They locked eyes again, not really staring, but Naya was focusing on keeping quiet and not starting the cycle of self-sabotage. She kept her tour groups small on purpose, giving up the chance to earn more for no good reason, really.

Consistency of character. That's the reason.

Still, she needed the money. Money literally walked into her van. She shouldn't toss it out on the street.

"Welcome to the tour, Ben," she said. "I think you'll end up enjoying yourself today."

"I doubt that," he replied. "But it won't be your fault at all."

Wow. Naya bit her lip. She should stop talking altogether, before she said anything she regretted. She was more mature now, and responsible. She gave him a stiff nod before she backed out of the van and left him in there.

Outside, she found herself face to face with her cousin Melly, "income-generating hobby" partner and her driver for the day.

"He's not part of the tour," Melly hissed, pointing at their stowaway. "Did he think we were his Uber or something?"

"He's part of it now. He paid and everything."

"But he didn't do the online form. We didn't vet him, and if there was an open slot we should have given it to the waitlist—"

"Melly," Naya sighed. "It's okay."

"You think? It's us and a bunch of strangers in a van—we should make sure we're safe—"

"I know who he is, Melly. It's okay."

Her cousin blinked at her. "He's a friend?"

She shook her head. "Not a friend. But he's...I recognize him. From work. I mean, the old job. I don't think he'll be a safety risk for us, and he already paid."

The difference between them was that Melly did not need this "job" as much and deferred often to Naya's decisions. "Okay," she said. "But I'll keep an eye on him just in case."

"Funny you said that—he seems to want to disappear today."

"So joining your See This Manila tour is the best thing for him today—or the worst."

"Depending on what he's trying to avoid. It shouldn't bother us. Let's carry on, have a great time as usual. Yes?"

Of course she was going to have a great time. She'd make sure of it. And whatever Benjamin Cacho—speechwriter working for the office of Senator David Alano—was hiding from, she was not going to let it affect her day at all.

2
***

It was going to be a long day, so Ben Cacho loaded up on podcasts before putting his mobile phone on airplane mode. Yes, airplane mode, as if he was taking a long-haul flight, but a rush hour ride from Makati to Quezon City was close enough. As he stood there with all his work things in the middle of a parking lot, he heard someone mention the van's destination, and figured that was as good a place as any to figure out where to go next. He thought it was a shuttle terminal, to be honest. He didn't realize it was a tour van, that he'd need to pay the equivalent of a round-trip flight out of Manila, but anyway. It wasn't even eight in the morning and he was on the road to nowhere, and he just gave the Strict Teacher all his money.

Wait—he had another phone. He wasn't totally off the grid. It was office-issued and only took calls, but that didn't count. It was always in his bag and on silent anyway. It wasn't set to vibrate, was it? He could feel his bag, on the floor but touching him through the legs of his jeans. To be safe, he laid the laptop backpack down flat and pushed it under the seat in front of him.

The first podcast was a French language lesson on food. Ben had subscribed to this a lifetime ago, when he thought he had time to learn French, or go anywhere that would make it useful. But the podcast promised ten-minute bursts of learning and it made him feel that he was progressing even when he still went nowhere near France.

He thought Naya the Strict Teacher would fill up the van but by the time six people had hopped in, she took a seat in the back with them, closest to the door. Then she signaled the van to leave.

Eight-ten, like she said.

La carte, s'il vous plaît?

"...glad I didn't have to leave anyone behind today," Naya the tour guide was saying. "I've done that before..."

Avez-vous un ménu en anglais?

"...the 'Filipino time' excuse is bullshit, and it's an insult to those like me who value my time and yours, period. I'd really appreciate it if it's not used to make yourself feel better for being late, or feel superior for being early..."

Ben laughed, and when everyone else turned to look at him he realized that he did so louder than he'd planned to. Earphones, damn. He meant to tune out the tour and disappear in the back, but—

"And that's Ben," Naya said, eyebrow raised. "Everyone, say hi to Ben. He's a sudden addition to our tour today."

"Hi, Ben," the others obediently said.

He touched his cheek, tried to push the smile away. He didn't need to be nice to anyone; he needed to ride this van and end up away from Makati. But soon everyone had turned around and the focus of attention was back where it deserved to be, Naya.

Vins rouges, vins blancs.

Ben felt some of his stress subsiding already, at about the rate of ten kilometers per hour. It was...nice? To not have to think of work for once. He kind of panicked when faced with hours and hours of being by himself and the first thing he did was pick up on things he had left off...three years ago. Was he even the same person? Did he actually want to learn *Français*?

"...modern art and actually experience it. Lunch will be at Chef Grace's family's home..."

He told himself not to pay attention, but lunch? He paid for lunch? Thank God, he was getting something to eat at least. He could figure out where to go after that.

"I'm sorry," he said, interrupting her spiel, but he couldn't help himself. "Is that Chef Grace Bayona?"

Naya paused and sighed, and he could imagine her telling herself to calm down. Inwardly. Outwardly she was poised and collected, the edge of her ponytail swishing and landing over one shoulder. "Yes, it is, Ben. You'd know that if you read the tour schedule, but yes, lunch will be at Chef Bayona's."

He'd met the chef once before, and remembered loving the food and promising to come back. Good day to get it done, then.

Je voudrais eau pétillante, s'il vous plait.

Ben tried to go back to learning a new language, he did. Then he just wasn't anymore, because the podcast ep had ended and he was looking at his tour guide, like everyone else in the van. He couldn't help it. She went on to explain several other tour destinations, not that it mattered because he wasn't going to be sticking around for the rest. Ben had been on tours before and even when they were mildly interesting, he could still retreat into silence. Naya was...he looked. Stole a glance here and there. Ended up listening. She acted like she was doing all of them a favor, that they had the honor of being in her van today, listening to her speak. For him she kind of did do him a favor for real, and yet everyone else seemed to act that way too.

"...now that I've told you where we're going," she said, "I want to thank you for deciding to spend the day with me. This is not what people usually think of, when they say they want to go around Manila, and if you're the right kind of restless that you ended up with me, then we could be—we could be friends."

Their eyes locked again when she said that last part, and of course that wasn't for him. He didn't count. He didn't choose her today; he was not the "right kind of restless." He was restless all right, but probably the wrong kind.

"Make no mistake, it'll still be Manila," Naya continued. "We'll pass through the same streets, crawl through the same traffic. We're not going to be driving through better neighborhoods just so you don't see the mess. It's still what it is, but you'll have your art, and food, and you'll see how supporting one artist helps the community. Hopefully you'll like what you see. Welcome to See This Manila. Wear your seatbelt and take a nap if you like. ETA for the next stop is nine-fifteen a.m."

She turned around, away from him, and it dawned on Ben that he knew her.

He knew Naya Llamas. Or rather, knew *of* her work, he was almost entirely sure now. He'd read those words before, or maybe heard them from her very mouth, except back then she was just another face at work.

What was she doing running a tour out of a van?

∼

"HI, BEN."

He did not expect he'd be spoken to by anyone else before the next stop, so it took him a while to respond. The lady occupying the seat right in front of him had turned around, the look on her face expecting a lot more than a hello back. She was waiting to be recognized.

On any other day, Ben would have gotten it right. That was his talent, his thing, what his boss needed him for on most days. *Who is this person and what is our history with this person?* He would use a face or a name as a starting point and his brain would map the beginnings of the "file" and he'd only really need the web research to fill in the blanks. Working for David—Senator Alano—taught him to build the mental file in reverse chronological order. What did that person say *yesterday*? In their world of shifting allegiances, that mattered more than what anyone did last month, last year, last election.

"I'm your Tita Mari," she said, beating him to it. "Second cousin of your dad. And this is—"

"Rochelle," Ben said, catching up. "Your daughter. Now in college, right?"

"Very good, Ben."

As the mental file began to form, he recalled one particularly stark memory of Tita Mari. He was ten years old, reciting Philippine presidents in sequence, along with their years in office. A reunion party trick the grownups made him do. "*Very good, Ben.*"

"Thank you," he said, also a programmed response.

"Going on this tour was Rochelle's idea," Tita Mari went on, never mind if the earphones were still in both his ears. "She's really into art and culture right now."

"None of my friends want to join a tour on a school break," Rochelle piped in, prepping her own earphones.

"You need better friends," Ben told her.

"I know, right?" Rochelle needed no other reaction to that, and had plugged into her own entertainment now.

"Just you?" Tita Mari said.

"Just me."

"Why just you?"

Ben shrugged. "I like art and culture."

"Rochelle is a fan of Naya the tour guide. I didn't even know that was a thing? How do you become a fan of a tour guide?"

"She did more than guide tours, before," Ben said. "Naya was part of a campaign to promote tourism." He wasn't even online so he couldn't fill the blanks, so he was going by stock knowledge here. If he knew of her work, then there could have been only a few projects they could have tangentially worked on together. Process of elimination yielded the handful that she could have directly participated in. Everything he said was true as long as he wasn't asked for specifics.

"That's amazing. She seems very passionate about it. Though I didn't realize she'd be that old."

Old? "She's probably around my age, Tita." He was thirty-two, but yes, that was old for some. He didn't need that additional bit of reflection, today of all days.

"Not that way, Ben. Rochelle watches her on YouTube and I thought they'd all be teenagers. Kids."

"Oh in that case, she's definitely not a kid."

"I'm glad to see you here, Ben. You seemed to be so buried in work the past few years."

His "work" and everything about it was now crammed into a backpack that was right under Tita Mari's seat. His work was now buried under her, in a way. He was surprised she hadn't mentioned any news from today, but maybe she was being polite. Or Naya was just that absorbing that Tita Mari hadn't felt the need to tune her out by going online. He had to remember to thank Naya even for the things she didn't know she was doing.

"Maybe I need better friends too," Ben said.

3

G uests of See This Manila probably thought Naya was aimlessly goofing off on the internet, during those lulls between tour stops and she was on her phone. She was, instead, browsing the guest profiles, reading the information they chose to share when they signed up to join her tour.

Mari and Rochelle Martinez, mother and daughter. Naya knew Rochelle; they'd started interacting online over a year ago. Rochelle was a frequent commenter on Naya's videos and posts, and had been trying to arrange to join a tour for a while. Naya scheduled her tours on weekdays so full-time students like Rochelle weren't often available, but this was a rare convergence of the right tour, the right schedule, and a week-long school break for her. It was nice of her mother to come along.

The other pair, Anil and Jana, were foreign nationals working at an international development organization. It was Anil's idea to join the tour and there were originally two other people from their workplace who reserved spots. But anyway, eventually only Anil and Jana showed up, and Naya was almost sure they'd be dating soon. If this wasn't the first date already. Showing up was crucial, she learned, when it came to dating. Even just emotionally.

She glanced over their profiles and told herself to be happy for them. An unexpected market for her tours? Couples. New couples. First or second date-type couples. She wasn't sure who gave people that idea but every tour she ever did had at least one couple, even when she planned to take them to places where they'd get hot, or sweaty, or dirty.

God maybe that's it. Haha, you people.

The third pair, Dexter and Danny, were an actual couple. She would never admit it but she kept a tally of cutest group in each tour, and the Dexter/Danny pair were the cutest today. Sorry, others. On their signup form, Dexter had said that it was their anniversary. Naya made sure to tell those in charge at their food stops to set up a nicer table than usual for them. They seemed pleasant and in a good mood but really, an anniversary wasn't to be spent with six other strangers at a table.

Wait, seven strangers now, because Ben.

Before leaving the parking lot that morning, Melly had pulled her into a quick conference outside the van.

"I looked him up."

"Ben?"

"Yes. I didn't want to leave without checking."

"That's great of you, and that's why we're partners. What's he hiding from?"

Melly had scrunched her nose in disgust. She didn't particularly like anything political. "Do you know anything about Senators Alano and Buena?"

She had tried to remember, but her background knowledge was almost zero on the current sitting senators, especially the ones who got their seats in the most recent election. Naya had been out of government consulting by then and wasn't paying attention. Only that David Alano and Jacqueline Buena were somewhat popular, and maybe insulted each other in the press at some point.

It was all the same to Melly. "I don't really understand it, but there's drama, and the two senators were arguing about something, and there's a statement that it's his fault and he's being let go from his position."

"You read an article on this?"

"I read a headline and the first paragraph. I really don't understand what else is going on here."

As described, that was a slow day in national politics, but as long as Melly didn't seem concerned, Naya was fine. They decided that they'd let him stay in the van, and the morning would go as scheduled.

Naya wasn't doing government work anymore, and even when she was, it was different from Ben's side of it. She was a traveler with a background in video production. Eventually she became part of a team that traveled and made videos of their travels to promote local tourism. Her interactions with politicians were kept to a minimum, but she was aware of personnel movement and chismis because that sometimes affected their side of things.

Since quitting her job, Naya avoided the news as much as she could. She tried to filter her news so she would only get tourism- and traffic-related things, and that wasn't much help because those two were connected to everything else. She didn't even know what to look for, but as soon as the news page began to load, she saw it.

Oh boy.

Well, Ben Cacho hadn't committed a crime. It was political drama, more like theater than real life. Melly shrugging it off was the exact reaction to be expected from regular people who considered all those guys the same kind of crooked and didn't care if a career ended today or not.

Looked like Ben's career ended today, within ten minutes of him stepping into her van, and that was the political life sometimes. But Naya knew what the other side of an epic career meltdown looked like and she survived it.

Ben would be fine. Maybe she should be nicer to him.

She looked his way, his corner at the back of the van.

He turned her way, a moment after, and caught her looking.

He smiled, mouth moving as if singing along to a thing coming from his earphones, and she wondered if she should feel sorry for him at all.

And why was she even thinking about him? This was time better spent on her actual tour guests, the ones who *wanted* to be there.

≈

QUEZON CITY, 9:45 a.m.

IF NAYA TURNED INTO A MONSTER, or if she actually were a monster right that minute, her eyes would be red. Red, burning, big eyes—so judgmental and *red*. The other monsters would probably stay away from her because *whoa that one, so red*.

The first stop of that day's See This Manila tour was the Arande Art Gallery in Quezon City, and they arrived within five minutes of Naya's original estimate. Now, Naya did not have a background in modern art, but she did know the curator, and in her humble opinion she thought this exhibit was fucking good.

She even had a favorite piece. After she spent some time introducing the gallery and checking the status of the art class collaboration she had set up, she went straight for it. The artwork was, to explain it simply, an entire wall of monsters. The artist did a "monster a day" webcomic project and the result, three hundred sixty-five colorful monsters, which were now on display, rows upon rows of them, against an off-white background. One monster was just three inches tall and had two heads. Another was twice as tall and had a fire in his belly—or instead of a belly.

Ben was already there, earphones thrown over his shoulder. He was bending forward, his eyes on the bottom row of monsters.

"So which one are you?" That was her standard line whenever someone from the tour joined her in looking. It was fun, and people laughed. Perfect ice-breaker.

Ben did not laugh. He smiled, but it was rueful, and he pointed to a monster holding its own head over its balls. "That one."

"Oh my God, Ben."

"I'm not too proud to admit it."

"Yes that seems to be a thing with you. Are you okay? Should you be somewhere else right now?"

"All I need is a moment. This moment, in front of these monsters, like I'm looking at the entrance to hell. And the Chef Bayona meal later that I'm sure will turn my life around."

"Ben." Naya needed to be the designated adult at her tour sometimes, and this was one of those moments. "I don't know if my tour is the right place for you to be...processing what's happened."

"Oh, so you know."

"Yeah. And I can give you your money back—"

"What did it say?"

"What?"

"The news. Whatever you read. What did it say?"

"It's a mess."

"Of course it is; it's politics. What did it say I did?"

"It said that the office of Senator Jacqueline Buena found out about a leaked message thread, where David Alano's camp conspired to release negative press on her private life during the campaign."

"Yes. And?"

"That you, Ben, suggested an attack on her looks, her first marriage, her child."

"Is that all?"

"*Is that all?*"

"That's not a long enough article. What else did it say?"

"That the negative campaign was killed and you never used it but now that the thread was leaked, Buena's asking for consequences and your resignation. That Alano's chief of staff confirmed that you gave it, last night."

"That's what it said? Elmo Laranas confirms I resigned last night?"

"How much of it is true?"

Ben shrugged. "It's the news. I guess it's true."

"Ben," she said, trying to keep her voice level. "Part of the reason why my tour is still just a 'hobby'? So I don't have to put up with shit. Don't lie to me while you're here."

"I guess you would understand, right? If I had to talk to anyone today."

"Excuse me?"

"You worked for PH Lens, didn't you?"

Yes, she did, but it wasn't officially called "PH Lens."

That was the internal nickname for the tourism project she consulted on for years, was her best job, also her most heart-breaking one.

Ben continued, "Of course it's not called PH Lens now, even if the office is intact, because everyone in the steering committee is new and it was written over at some point. I would know that because David Alano was in the original committee, all those years ago, and I was already in his team then. Before the elections, of course."

"You know who I am. Did you know when you got in the van?"

"No. But I figured it out when you started talking about 'Filipino time.' I was like, damn I've heard this before. I know this rant."

"Well." She looked down at her shoes, then across to the monsters. Sure she did video and for years had her face in front of the camera, but this felt like a different kind of exposure. Most days, she didn't interact with former work people. When she did, it felt like they knew a side of her that she wasn't sure if she should hide.

Worlds collide, and all.

"Some days I'm that monster," Naya said, pointing to the one with flowers growing out of its head. "Insides hanging out oddly, and still a monster."

"That's beauty," Ben said earnestly. "It's not odd at all."

"Do I need to call you a car to take you home, Ben? I can do that. I think I should."

"No. I'm being honest here. I'd rather not be home. I'd rather be outside, looking at monsters. I'd rather talk to you. I'd rather eat a good meal before I retreat to joblessness. This is...this is nice."

Briefly, Naya wondered if she should loop Melly in, ask

her to decide whether to ship Ben off or not. But then she pointed to a different monster. "This should be you."

He squinted at it. "You think."

It was wearing a hat and carrying a ball of fire in its hand. "We're all still monsters but we can do it with fashion."

"And fire. Will you let me stay in the tour, Naya?"

"Yes. If you behave yourself."

4

Before officially joining the office of then-congressman David Alano, Ben and art galleries were not a thing. He had gone through childhood, college, law school, intermittently interning for Rep. Alano, and one year of working at a non-profit focusing on child health without stepping inside one. Then his political life began and it was like he'd been inside every single gallery in Metro Manila.

His boss had ties with patrons of the arts, and there was always an invitation to an exhibit, a gallery, art in the park, the opera. Sometimes, on blessed days, Ben didn't have to go, but when he went, he had to admit that he learned a few things.

Ben wanted to live that way, wanted to think that even when he was bored out of his mind he had at least improved himself.

David Alano was an intelligent, well-educated, principled man and still managed to not act like a prick. People born with that kind of likeability were rare. Still, Ben noticed how his boss's demeanor changed the slightest bit, depending on his audience. How he was with a billionaire philanthropist, with generals, with the press, with his constituents. Ben picked up on subtle changes in his words, his tone, and as someone whose primary function was writing speeches, all these became useful.

Not that he had any fun doing any of that.

But none of that today. No art patrons to woo, no political society to schmooze. In fact, no job in politics even. Just him and art, and maybe that tour guide who was watching him like a hawk.

There was a chair inside a red cubicle with three walls, and the sign invited him to sit. He did, so obedient of him, and he tried not to think of hygiene and all the other people who did the same thing because they too followed the sign. Sit and press the black button, it said, and the red wall in front of him came to life as light projected on it.

Today is the day
Today my life begins
Today in history
Today is holiday

The phrases kept flashing, one after another, each one in a handwritten scrawl or elaborate cursive. *Today is. Today is.* Ben wasn't sure what it was supposed to accomplish, but today he had a headache. Still, he sat for the entire cycle, because he was like that. The last screen of text that flashed at him told him to go to the small desk and write down what today meant to him.

There was a white card and a Sharpie, and Ben didn't have to think about it for very long.

Today sucks because I suck.

He'd find work, eventually. Shouldn't be a problem, right? Someone would have a use for a thirty-two-year-old lawyer who didn't want to be a lawyer and was formerly a speechwriter, right? He couldn't imagine just yet what or who, only that with the great many things that sucked in the world, there surely would be something for him to help fix.

Though would that be the best thing, because maybe he'd find himself right in this spot again.

"We're leaving in five minutes," Naya said, coming up behind him and already wearing her little backpack. "In case you wanted to do anything here, last minute."

"I'm fine."

"Really? Don't want to go around more?"

"I was here at this gallery's opening and I recognize the stuff. Most of it anyway."

"Oh *excuse me*. Perhaps you need to use the bathroom?"

"No."

"Or I don't know...change your Today statement?"

"But that *is* how I feel about 'today.'"

Naya was cute when she was exasperated. He still knew better than to say that aloud. She tried to stare him down and he wasn't sure what to say, except that he did want to get out of her way but all of the ways were hers and he couldn't seem to get out.

"I'm ruining the vibe today, is that it?" Ben said. "Are we supposed to be super I Love Manila hearts and rainbows?"

"Not at all." Something that he said must have pushed a button too, because she frowned and also stepped back, giving up on the stare-down. He didn't mean to offend her. Truth was he didn't get a lot of sleep and now that the fatigue was setting in, the words were slipping out. Leaking.

"I'm sorry," he said quickly. "And there's nothing wrong with hearts and rainbows."

"Damn right. You should know how hard it is, for a lot of people these days."

"Yes, yes I do."

"You should know that it flat-out *sucks* for people to walk around daily knowing that they have to guard their right to live all the freaking time."

He winced. "I'm sorry."

But he started something and she wasn't done. "You *of all people* should know that the strength to get up in the morning and face another trash day might be coming from knowing that there are still regular people who do great things and it helps to remind others that these people exist because we hurt them twice by being ignorant of their existence. Right?"

"Of course. I really am sorry."

The words leaked out of Naya too; obviously this was an anger that was very well articulated, already in her head, probably constantly. She gave him a once-over, and it was like she stopped herself from saying more. "Okay then. Wanting hearts and rainbows during these times is a perfectly valid response to trash world."

"I understand, yes."

Then she let out a long breath. "That said, I'm perfectly aware Manila's a hard sell even when things are good. Plus we're absolute experts at *I'm sorry my house is shit, come inside, have you eaten*. I can't change a thing about that. So... now we're going to lunch."

"Look at mine!" The voice came from one of the guys from the tour, and his timing would have been better a minute ago, but Ben was going to take it. The guy was holding his card up to Ben and Naya. *Today is the first day of the rest of our lives.*

"Dexter," Naya whispered, taking the card out of his hands. Were the cards supposed to be secret? Not that anyone watched Ben be all moody with his. "You're sure about this?"

"Yes. Yes. I'm sorry I took forever." Dexter was serious about his statement.

Naya smiled, and it seemed warmer when it was directed at someone else. "All right. Let me just close up here? You two can head to the van now."

At least the dismissal wasn't just for Ben, so he took it, and walked with Dexter in the direction of the driveway of the gallery. They were the last of the group to leave the building, it seemed—everyone else was already back in the van.

"So, did you do it?" Dexter asked him.

Ben couldn't even *hide* properly, could he? No one cared who Ben was, frankly, throughout his career. Any instincts he had were trained to help his boss, or a project, or an advocacy. His own survival skills needed a lot of work. "Did I do what?"

"Get fired for engaging in dirty politics."

"Probably." And maybe he shouldn't have said that to a stranger just now, but it was already an odd day. "What do you do, Dexter?"

"Advertising...which has its own dirt and politics. But you're on the hot seat now."

Ben shrugged. "I did get fired, and all politics is dirty. So...yes?"

"I thought David Alano was one of the better ones."

If he were on the job, that comment would have been considered a gold star. A complicated one, but they didn't get anything in black and white anyway. If anyone thought David was principled, that was a good enough start. This time the implication was that he wasn't, and Ben felt the sting even now.

"He is," Ben couldn't help but say. "I was an intern for him for a while before I joined his staff. That's years of watching him work. I wouldn't have been able to continue as I did if I didn't believe he's one of the better ones. And see it myself."

"But you're here now," Dexter said. "Unemployed. And that thing they leaked? The basis of the attack on Buena's campaign? That's low. It's sexist as fuck. Not the best look from someone who's supposed to be better."

"That's not him. It really isn't."

"Is it you?"

Ben sighed. But did he have to? Who the hell was he protecting even? "It's not me. I have no power or connections so if there's anyone who gets to be thrown under the bus, I'm the best candidate. No one will miss me. *But* any dirty political player will say the exact same thing so you probably won't believe me, and that's your right, Dexter."

"Well you're cheerful," Dexter said.

She found him in the kitchen, arranging wide-mouth glasses on a tray.

Naya thought she had settled in everyone in the tour group for lunch, then noticed she had lost her extra guy. He wasn't at the dining room, or the van. Maybe he left and didn't say goodbye?

Not that he had to say goodbye. He didn't *owe* her anything. She'd have to give him *his* money back, even, if he skipped half the tour. But he wasn't out there on the driveway of the Bayona home, so Naya went back inside.

And found him in the kitchen.

"He paid for the lunch, Chef," Naya said. "You don't need to put him to work."

Chef Grace laughed, and so did her new "assistant." Ben had taken off his blazer and maybe undid the top button of his shirt and rolled up his sleeves...whatever the change, it was a more casual look. Less "legislative branch."

"I know this young man, Naya," the chef said, placing a bowl of calamansi in front of him. "I'm sure he doesn't mind helping out."

Chef Grace had always been Tita Grace to Naya. Grace Bayona and Naya's mom were lifelong friends. Naya remembered occasional Sunday meals at this very place, home to the chef and her parents and siblings. Those siblings and Chef Grace eventually chose to live elsewhere, and the large house in Quezon City served only to host larger family reunions. In some cases, private meals, like the one Naya arranged for her tours.

Naya loved this kitchen too. Large and *old*. The oven-and-range set was shiny and new, but the white-and-blue tiles and painted-over brick were from back in the day. The counter in the middle had a new surface but it was the same island for food prep. She would grab a mango or an orange from the fruit basket when she saw one—they never had fresh stuff at home so it was such a novelty.

"I like helping out," Ben said. "You need me to slice these?"

"In half, like this." Chef Grace sliced one citrus globe in half with a small knife, then handed him both the knife and the chopping board. "I'll need them later for something."

This wasn't standard procedure, but...at least Ben was getting something to do? She parked herself on a stool by the counter as she tried to wrap her brain around this. "So how do you know Ben, Chef?" she said, pulling a grape from the counter and popping it into her mouth.

"Was it five years ago?" Chef Grace turned around from sending the appetizers out and joined them back at the counter. "Fundraiser for that livelihood center. I catered that."

"*Four* years," Ben corrected her, though his attention seemed to be on the calamansi. "I had just formally joined the senator's staff. But he was in congress at the time." He paused in his slicing and laughed, to himself like he was remembering a past love, and Naya's heart broke a little. "Seems like a long time ago."

Then she reminded herself that it shouldn't. One didn't mourn the loss of a job that made them compromise their principles. If they missed the position, it was because they were probably earning something off it, and not the above-board salaries because those were measly compared to what they could have been getting elsewhere. It meant they were probably cheating the people, or wasting those hard-earned taxes at the very least. Ben shouldn't be sad—this was the beginning of the rest of his life.

"You hid in the kitchen!" The memory came to Chef Grace right that second, and Ben flinched. "Now I remember how I met you."

"No, we met when David introduced us. I was his new speechwriter."

"I don't remember anyone that way. *You* went right into the kitchen and offered to do things. Like right now. That's how we met."

"Well that's why Chef Grace likes you," Naya said. "She likes volunteers."

He was blushing. Was he blushing? Did slicing cala-mansi induce a reaction that made one's forehead and cheeks a little pink? Of course not. Ben Cacho was blushing. Also very intently slicing, evading this topic of conversation as much as he could. "I get weird around some people, that's all."

She popped another grape in her mouth. They didn't need her outside yet, did they? Melly would be calling for her if she was needed. "Who was at this fundraiser, Chef?"

The main course was Chef Grace's kare-kare and she had begun ladling single-serving portions into wide bowls. It smelled divine, and Naya instantly wanted to curl up into one of the bowls and have the peanut stew poured all over her. Chef Grace, she knew, remembered things through food too. "I served nilaga that day. I remember, because that's what Ben helped me with."

"I love that nilaga too, Tita," Naya said.

"And banana fritters. And...oh it was the event with the Vice President. Several bank presidents."

"Only the fanciest people eat Chef Grace's food, right?"

"I remember David especially. So handsome. And he sounded so smart. He was talking to this beautiful lady...I think she was with some NGO..."

"I think I should help you do that instead," Ben said. No, he *demanded* it, and he all but grabbed the ladle from the chef's hand. But he was too quick, and he set down his paring knife a little too quickly, so it spun in a circle on his chopping board and slid toward Naya.

"Oh my God!" Naya said.

"Naya!" said Chef Grace.

It looked scary but Naya had it under control, for sure. She had jumped out of the way of the spinning knife right on time *and* she had knocked it toward a safer trajectory and a full stop using the bowl of grapes.

She couldn't say the same for her Tita Grace, whose hand holding the ladle also tried to reach for the knife, and instead flung kare-kare sauce on the counter—and Ben. Ben's hand, Ben's forearm, Ben's nice work shirt.

"I'm so sorry," Ben said. "Chef. I shouldn't have—I'm sorry."

"No one's hurt?" Chef Grace asked, but she was looking at Naya, who tried to make light of it by checking her fingers.

"All complete," she said. "Ben, don't worry. I have a shirt for you to wear."

~

IF BEN KNEW what he had signed up for that day, he would
know that he was really actually going to get a shirt. Part of
the tour and the *Today* statement exhibit was an activity
involving students of the gallery's ongoing watercolor and
calligraphy workshop. Their visit was scheduled and timed
precisely on a class day, and Naya had arranged for the
students to get their first commission—creating art from the
"today" statements of her tour group and printing it onto
shirts for the tour guests to take home as a souvenir. The
idea was suggested on one of Naya's visits, and they set up
the process for it pretty quickly, and tested it on her next
tour. She lived for this kind of collaboration, and loved
when it landed on her lap because people wanted it to
happen, and made it happen, instead of writing letters to
layers of powers that be.

No one liked doing that. Ugh, it made her skin crawl just
remembering how she had to turn each idea into a piece of
paper, how it always morphed into something a little bit
different, to fit someone else's agenda.

Ugh.

The "today" shirts meanwhile—that was a fun project,
and quick to execute. The designs were produced within the
hour class period, then immediately photographed, printed,
and transferred onto shirts that were sent over by motorbike
courier to Chef Bayona's house, arriving just as they finished
their appetizer course. Which was great timing because
Naya and Ben had stayed behind in the kitchen while the
chef talked her guests through what to expect for lunch.

Naya cut open the courier package and searched inside
for Ben's shirt. She saw it, and giggled. It was his statement

all right, but in beautiful cursive, framed by gorgeous, *large*, red flowers.

Today sucks because I suck.

"Here," she said.

He looked at it and she heard the sound of ironic pain. "Wow."

"I told you, you're getting a shirt."

"This truly is mine." Ben unfolded the gray round-neck shirt, and held it up to get a full view of the art. He had to hold it gingerly, and very far from his body. He had washed his hands and arms but his shirt still had a kare-kare stain, a brown-orange blotch on the left side near the waist and another on the left sleeve around the elbow. "It's beautiful though."

"Of course it is. The artist is credited on a little card in the bag."

"I...I'm probably going to send the artist a thank-you note. This truly is art out of my crap. It's as confused about itself as I am."

"I gave you a chance to change your statement."

"No," Ben said, with more conviction. "It's the truth."

He set the shirt down on the corner of the counter and began undoing his buttons with the same conviction, and Naya blinked, but did not look away. Then he was shirtless, very fit, a little sweaty and red like he had blushed all the way underneath his clothes. Shirtless right there in the chef's kitchen.

"I don't think you're supposed to do that here." It came out as a stage whisper, hushed but not enough.

He had caught her looking. "I've made you uncomfortable."

She realized that she maybe shouldn't have been caught

looking. "Well I just meant it's a kitchen. Sanitation rules, I'm sure."

"Of course. I'll—" He motioned to the door to the "dirty kitchen" in the back, when really he could have just worn the shirt on the spot, and now spent more seconds walking around without a shirt.

Naya pushed another grape into her mouth to keep another giggle in. Thirty-one years old and on the job; she shouldn't spend this much time giggling. And ogling.

Today is the day.

6

"Nice shirt."

Ben smiled at his Tita Mari. "Thank you."

He joined them at their table set for seven, assuming that the empty spot was for him. Tita Mari and her daughter, Melly the driver, Naya, the two who weren't Filipinos, and him. Dexter and the other guy, and he was assuming they were a couple, were sharing a smaller table closer to the large window. The discussion was lively and thankfully about another topic altogether, and he was able to sit down and start eating without having to say much.

He could not believe he sacrificed a good shirt for essentially nothing. Old habits died maybe never. He was going to have to learn to do some killing.

The fundraiser that Chef Grace was talking about, he did remember that. It was one of the first society events of that level he'd had to attend, and he hadn't yet mastered how to handle himself when introduced to this celebrity, that rich person, those politicians. Ben could handle himself when speaking in public, or saying complete sentences to an important person. Just...there had been a *lot* of them in one place, you know? It was a bit much. Chef Grace seemed to understand that, and she let him stay in the kitchen, and do random things like sort napkins and stack glasses.

Then he went and ruined it, the theme of the day really, when the chef mentioned Tana, and Ben's instinct of keeping that quiet kicked in. Well, Tana's name hadn't been said, but David and the lady from the NGO? That was Tana Cortes, and Ben went right into *we don't talk about Tana* mode.

Which was for nothing, really. Not just because Ben no longer had that job, but seriously, who the fuck cared if the senator liked the woman? He was single, and people expected him to date and marry and all that.

Because it's complicated. All the right answers, work-related, came pouring in, because Ben knew all this in his mind but he also knew that fuck all that, did it even matter. They had so many rules to follow at work; he had to get used to not having to follow them.

Still, one of his best work shirts had kare-kare spots on it now. And for what.

"This is good," he said, to no one in particular, as he ate. "Definitely better in my stomach than on my clothes."

"And this is considered comfort food, right?" someone at the table asked.

"Yes, Anil," Naya answered. "Chef Bayona's family is known for comfort food, the kind we eat at holidays and celebrations."

"I love that, about your food trip videos," Rochelle said. "I'm just as sick as you are of the stunt food, like when they bring something out just to gross out the tourists."

Ben remembered that, again, from his short exposure to that project she was in. A debate precisely about the stunt food, whether making videos about them was cute or perpetuated stereotypes. It had divided the teams, somehow escalated to his boss's desk, and David told him to form the reply. They said no to funding videos of white people being freaked out by balut.

"If you want balut, or fried insects, we can do that," Naya said, her tone measured. "There are people who seriously enjoy them, and make them. If you're going to ask for them so you can make a face and insult those who make them and eat them, I'm not here for it."

"Well, this kare-kare is perfect. Is this available at the chef's restaurant?" Tita Mari asked the tour guides.

"No," Naya said. "Our lunch today is off-menu, but if she caters for you one day maybe you can ask for any of these."

"Naya knows the most awesome people," Rochelle gushed to her mother, but the entire table was witness to it. "She knows chefs, surfers, those guys who protect forests and animals, people who work in hotels, everyone! On my birthday last year, we went to Bacolod and I did half the things I saw on her videos and it was all awesome."

"Naya fangirl," Tita Mari explained, unnecessarily at that point. "Naya knows Ben too, from work. Small world."

Naya cleared her throat. "Big world," she said, "but all connected. It gets easier to find people you need when you know who they work or collab with."

"And I'm not an awesome person," he said. "We don't get called awesome, in my line of work. We get called a lot of other names, but not that."

"Ben is an exception!" Tita Mari declared with so much conviction that Ben noted that it was a mistake being self-deprecating near her. "I've known him since he was a child and he's a sharp one. So talented and smart. So interested in history—which you know is rare for kids—and has an excellent memory. His parents were so proud of him."

Past tense, not because he had done something to lose that status, but because they had both already died within the last decade. Usually, remembering that fact ranged from painful to bittersweet, but right then he was relieved that they both didn't have to wake up to the news that he had resigned for suggesting a sexist and ultimately baseless attack on a rival candidate. He had never experienced parental discipline in his life, but he would have gotten an ear twisting and a lecture about respecting women's choices. He would also have to explain to both parents that he didn't fail them, but he happened to be the guy with the least political clout. The law degree, the years of loyal and hard work, memorizing all the presidents and reciting the sequence to astounded relatives...none of those mattered.

"Maybe," Ben said, shifting the conversation back where it should have stayed, "Naya knows awesome people because she is one, herself."

"You shouldn't throw that word around so casually. We just met," she told him.

"I'm going on evidence," Ben insisted. "And what seem to be sincere testimonials from at least three people here whom I've known for years and trust. It's rare to see this kind of passion and...care. For what this city has to offer."

"Naya's tour is highly recommended," the guy named Anil said. "It was on the list of things to do in the city given to me by my employer when I relocated to Manila."

"Really?" Both Naya and Melly said that, but Melly pulled out her phone and started taking notes. "When was this, Anil?"

"I moved eight months ago," he said. "There's an orientation we have to go through, about the culture, life in Manila, where to buy stuff, things to do. This was on the list."

"We didn't know that. We don't have a regular tour sked

with your company. If I had known that, we would have created one for you instead of slotting you into this one." Melly was talking. It was the business side of the operation, and Melly was doing the talking. Ben found this interesting, and glanced over at Naya to see if this was affecting her at all. She was eating, eyes down at her plate.

Were they partners because Melly handled the business side of things? Did Naya care about any other side? How much help did she need, to get this off the ground and keep it running? How long could she keep working like this, running a tour out of a van?

He was about to suggest something, but nah. Who was the jobless one? Him. No moral authority to suggest things.

"What's the coolest thing you saw Naya feature on her videos?" he asked Rochelle instead.

"Oh God, I can't name just one thing," Rochelle said. "But the dugong sighting would be in my top three!"

"Palawan," Naya added.

"That Manila on rooftops series," Rochelle continued. "She did a series of videos from different building rooftops around the city. Best rooftops and the best sunsets! That was so unexpected."

"Where's the best sunset?" Ben asked. "Or is it all the same? Anything by the bay, right?"

"Not necessarily," Naya said.

"Where then?"

Naya blinked at him. "You really want to know?"

"Of course."

"There's this hotel in Intramuros," she said. "I mention it in one of my videos. When you look out from the roof, you see old and new, everything really, and when it's orange and red and pink, it's extraordinary."

"Are we going there today?"

She shook her head. "Dinner is somewhere else."

Rochelle frowned at him. "You don't know where we're going today? You didn't go through the itinerary?"

Naya's smile tightened. "Ben wanted to be surprised. And I thought you just wanted to do half of the day."

"Don't waste it!" Rochelle said. "You don't do just *half* of a See This Manila tour! What's the point?"

"He doesn't have to do the whole thing, Rochelle. He might have other things to do."

"It's not easy to get on a tour, though!" Rochelle piped in. "The itinerary changes every time. And as soon as she announces one, the slots are filled up in like ten seconds. If you're already here you should stay the whole day, Kuya Ben. I mean, what else are you going to do today?"

Good question, Kuya Ben. If he went home he would mope. God forbid a friend from work might visit to check up on him, and he wanted none of their concern or good intentions.

"I'm staying," Ben said.

"You are?" Naya was surprised.

"I can't leave now," he said. "Since you're so highly recommended."

"You were lucky to get into this one, Ben," Tita Mari told him.

There was something about the way Naya looked at him. He felt it now, her face holding a slight smirk at him, sure. His brain was in a fog when he was changing his shirt, apparently in front of her, but he felt it too. That wasn't just the fog. She was in charge, but she wasn't uncaring. She didn't tell him to pack up and go home. He *was* lucky, he knew that now, and he had decided to stay where the luck was.

7

Taguig, 2:45 p.m.

"So I was talking to Anil and Jana, about that relocation package that our tour was mentioned in."

"Right. I mean yeah, I should have asked earlier. I lost track of things."

Melly shrugged. "No big. That's what I'm here for. Anyway, we could be contracted to do regular tours for them. They have budgets for team building and cultural immersion of international hires, stuff like that. But we need to be accredited."

Of course they did. Naya winced, and her cousin saw it.

"We should do it."

"I know we should. It's just...ugh."

"We talked about this, Naya. Next level."

"I know, I know."

"I have a deadline."

Melly was being nice about this, but Naya knew what it all meant. Next level, deadline, everything to do with taking this more seriously than the "income-generating hobby" it started out as. Melly was a business major, entrepreneurial by nature, and while super supportive, also kept reminding Naya that there should be a future to this or she would move on to other things. For the past year or so, Naya was able to hold her off by claiming paperwork aversion, residual pains from working with the government. It worked for a while.

Was it so bad, hanging on to freedom for a little while longer? Naya was lucky enough to be considered good at anything, and for people to agree to pay this kind of money for something she was passionate about...

It wasn't going to last, said everyone in her life who ever had a career and knew a thing about money. The real world would come calling eventually. This was a "business" that relied on Naya being alert and healthy otherwise no money got made.

But I like it that way. Stubborn, still. Naya liked that this was work that she made, that required her full presence and involvement. She was proud that it was hers from end to end, and that people could try to do it but it wouldn't be the same.

And most of all, she loved that she could walk away from it at any time.

"They like you," Melly said. "Anil and Jana like the tour and are willing to vouch for you, and they've only been to half of it. I'll email you the accreditation requirements. We should get this done as soon as we can."

What that would mean, in real world terms, was that Naya would have to formalize this somehow. Sign papers. Make herself available when they wanted tours. Plan her calendar around them, maybe a year or two in advance.

Real work. Because this wasn't work yet, even if she called it that, and even if it paid her bills.

"If they really needed someone to do this for them in-house, they can get someone who actually works in tourism. Already certified." She had to say it, and it wasn't just a deflection. She didn't want to take work away from anyone who'd been doing this as a career, carrying all the baggage of institutional decisions and misconceptions of what people wanted or needed. She presented herself as an alternative precisely so she could do it her way, and be free from all that.

"They asked for *you*. Obviously they wouldn't just take in the next applicant who can show them around the city."

"Fine," Naya said. "I'll look at it later."

"Promise?"

"Yes." She checked her watch. "We have time to walk through the park before heading into the rink. Can you direct the guests that way?"

Melly gave her a smirk but did as she asked, knowing she was being dismissed.

This was a good group, and Naya could have asked them to cross the street and walk through the park on her own. They would have done as she asked, and they did. She sensed a floating blur beside her and noticed that someone from the tour group didn't follow instructions. Of course.

"I hope you don't mind me asking," Ben said as he approached. "How long since you left PH Lens?"

"Three years." But as she thought about it, it was a little more than three years actually.

"Did you work somewhere else, after?"

"I wasn't doing anything for maybe eight months? Then I started making videos again, did some freelance work for prod houses."

Wow, she just did that. She just casually summarized a chaotic time in her life in a couple of sentences, like it was no big deal.

Ben had matched her pace, was now walking beside her as they crossed the street. "Was it an end-of-contract thing?"

She could tell him to mind his own business and join the rest. But instead: "No, not an end-of-contract thing. I walked into the office and yelled 'I fucking quit I am done with you all!' And then...that was it."

"Holy shit. You did?"

"Middle of a project, Ben. I'd have slammed a door except the door was heavy and one of those glass things that don't slam."

He laughed under his breath. "It's the dream."

"I don't have my last pay from that yet. Because...well it's hard to go back and sign the quitclaim when you've said you're fucking done."

"Now I feel I should have done that. That's a better exit."

Naya's group, led now by Melly, had made it to the Six 32 Central mall's park, and they seemed to know what to do with the sculptures on display. She turned her attention back to Ben. "Seems like you didn't have a choice what your exit would look like. And I thought David Alano was okay, considering everyone else is a two-faced liar and-or complicit in systemic hardship and death?"

"Please, don't sugarcoat on my behalf," he said dryly. "And you can still believe in David Alano, if you've given up on everyone else. He's a good guy."

"How can he be one, Ben? Or if he started out that way, how can he remain one in this environment?"

"He is, I promise. If you think my promises are worth anything. It's why everything's so hard for him, but that he's even gotten this far means people are beginning to hope again."

Oh dear. An optimist had walked into her van. Naya almost couldn't believe it; she was hanging out at a park with an optimist. How could he remain that after years of doing what he did, swimming in shark-infested waters? "Ben, that is hard to believe."

"But it's true. Ask me about any transaction, any committee he sat on, any position he had."

"I won't be doing that, because it's useless. You've been fired from the staff, so it doesn't matter if he's a superhero. It's either he's a good person or he's the jerk who threw you under the bus."

"I offered to quit, okay?" His glasses were bothering him for some reason, and he took them off and slipped them into the pocket of his blazer. "It looked like they were going to make that feud with Buena worse before it got better, so I offered to quit. I suggested this particular storyline, like what if the person to quit would be me. I didn't like the kind of work we were doing lately and I wanted a transfer maybe...but I also said it at two in the morning and I wasn't sure how quickly it would get out, if we'd get to sit down and talk about the details first."

The news websites had the resignation articles up first thing in the morning though. "I guess they...took your offer then."

"I guess they did. Lesson: don't send emails with incomplete sentences when you're sleepy. Years of loyal, competent service and I end a career with this. Also, it's fucking hot out here." He shrugged out of his blazer all together, and then it was just the *Today sucks because I suck* shirt—and too-good-for-the-blazer forearms and bicep action. "I only asked about your quitting because I wanted to know how long it could take me to find another job."

"Oh. That? Haha, it could take forever."

His face fell a little. "You're not kidding?"

"It won't take too long to find one, if you're willing to do anything. I don't think you'll be willing to *do anything*, Ben. You seem like a fella with principles."

"Yeah, look where those got me. I'll need to eat."

Naya didn't come from a family of civil servants, and she barely was one herself. What she had was a fierce love for the Filipino, loved what they created, wanted to make sure they got their due. She thought it was a dream, at first, getting paid to do exactly that, and for the ones in charge of taking care of the people. When she quit, all the help she got involved jobs outside tourism. She didn't have a mentor from within, no one to tell her what the future would look like had she stayed, or how she could go somewhere else and do the same thing.

Look at her now, being all mentory. "So I quit because I was deployed to do touristy videos during one of the summits. And I wanted to be assigned to Manila, because I thought it would be a good chance to show the inequality, what life is really like even on the days when they don't hide the shit from delegates traveling from the airport to wherever. I thought if I did it with some compassion, and with help from the communities themselves, I'd be able to create something and the summit would be the right platform for it. Because that's what it's for, right?"

"Oh, God," Ben said, realizing where this was going. "You had a dream too."

"I didn't even think I had one until someone told me to put on makeup and show my cleavage, and just take a video of the sunset, because that was the only thing they were paying me for." Damn. Saying it led to reliving it, and Naya felt the anger in her blood again. "The fuck, right? And sometimes I suspected that they'd only hired me to look pretty on camera, but they never said it, so I went on pretending they needed my point of view, my ideas."

"So you got the fuck out of there."

"Yes, I did. I don't know what it'll be like for you, but it's hard to fit my head into a certain mindset now. And I know I should be saving more, and earning more, and doing all those adult things but I also can't be bothered to kiss ass anymore. That kind of thinking leads one to this."

"A park in the middle of the day?"

"Milking your hobbies for money."

He might have gulped; she wouldn't be surprised. "It's possible I didn't think this through, when I offered to do this."

"Most people in government have rich families to help them out, I hear."

He shook his head. "Not me. I wonder which hobby of mine I can milk then."

If they took another step they'd be inside the park, and among the group, and maybe it was time to be folded back in to a happier space. "You can worry about that another day," she said. Without thinking much of it, she took his hand and pulled him under the ivy-covered arch. "Today you're on my clock, so you do what I say. It's time to take selfies with the horse sculptures and watch out for butterflies."

"Sounds amazing," Ben said.

She wasn't sure if he meant that, but he was just going to have to trust her. He wasn't going to have an easy road ahead, if hers was any indication.

8

He hopped into a random van to get away. Had he known it would lead to even more personal humiliation and possible injury, would he have done it differently?

"That's better," his tour guide said, putting more distance between them, but still holding his hand. "Is it coming back to you now?"

It was ice skating, something he did for five consecutive weekends when he was thirteen years old, and then never again. That was long enough for him to conclude that ice hockey wouldn't be in his future, never mind if he thought it would make him cooler. Not his first life lesson on literal and figurative, but it stuck, and he ended up working with words instead.

She didn't have to hold his hand. There were skate aids available—they looked like smartly-dressed polar bears, and people could hang on to one and push themselves on the ice and remain upright, if a little less dignified. But he stepped on the ice, then somehow this happened, and like no time at all they had gone around the rink once and the muscle memory was returning.

"You're good at this," Ben said.

Naya's smile a second ago had probably been at his expense, but it changed to being slightly pleased, possibly proud of herself. "I totally thought I was going to be a gold medalist figure skater when I was a kid."

"No other way to imagine it."

"I'm happy you understand." Naya skated with more confidence, her easy glides were likely the force that kept him upright. "It wasn't for me, eventually, but I've stayed in touch with Skating HQ. I like coming back here. And one of my friends from skate school eventually became the biggest deal."

"Calinda Valerio." Ben remembered her; she made national news when she won several medals during her time as a competitive skater.

"She's here. She'll be introducing the rehearsal we're watching." Her laugh sounded like it was bouncing off the ice and him. "But right, you didn't know that."

"I did say I wanted to be surprised? Did not think I'd be back on the ice today."

"You're doing okay."

Ben *was* doing okay. It took another couple of minutes to remember what it felt like, to use the blades to connect to the ice surface, to get comfortable with the forward motion, to go with the lack of friction instead of resist. Then it was better and he managed to correct his posture too...and then Naya let go of his hand.

"You're fine," she declared.

He was *cold*, was what he was. He wished he hadn't left his blazer in the locker area. Naya was ready and wearing a knit sweater that looked thick and comfortable. It was soft, too; he had been able to confirm that because the sleeve went all the way to the middle of her palm, that he'd been hanging onto for dear life earlier.

"Yes, I think I'll make it." A thirty-minute skating session wasn't going to kill him. "Why is skating part of the tour?"

"Because we're good at it."

"Because we win competitions?"

"I mean it's been around for a long time, and we've been able to train skaters and hockey players to win medals, and still the main point of any article written about them is *how cute tropical country with a rink.* It undermines what they're capable of, and what they're already doing, and it keeps people from investing emotionally in it because it's seen as a novelty."

No tour of the metro he even imagined taking would have this as a stop, that was true. Except Naya's, because she saw a different city. "How often is the rink part of your tour then?"

"This is the first time," Naya said. "You're lucky."

"I keep being lucky in oh so many ways."

She grinned. "That's the spirit. Cal works at the rink now and has a special project going on, and we get to see the rehearsal for it. Do you know what happens to figure skaters when they retire?"

Ben did not. Even the term "retirement" seemed odd, because his memory of Calinda Valerio was fairly recent, and she surely wasn't much older than they were. "They coach?"

"If they want to keep skating, they'll need to join a company, one that travels the world to do shows most likely. If they can't do that, or would rather not, they stay and coach. Or...they move on. Become nurses, engineers, moms, whatever they felt they put on hold to skate for the country."

Out of the corner of his eye, he saw them skate past where they came in, again. Twice around the rink now, and he was gaining confidence.

"Calinda's trying something new," Naya said. "Trying to create shows that people will pay to see, and made here. In-house team. Local skaters. All that. You'll see it later. And look at that, time's almost up."

Almost up? Right when he had gotten the hang of navigating on the slippery surface. He hadn't done a thing to impress her yet—not that he learned or remembered any tricks from before. Better to keep the injury count to zero.

~

EVENTUALLY HE DID GET to meet Naya's friend and national team for figure skating medalist Calinda Valerio. At thirty years old, she was the new creative director for Six 32 Central's rink, and their group was getting a special preview of an all-new project. For the next hour or so, they would be watching the technical rehearsal of their new show, an adaptation of *Ibong Adarna*. On ice.

He had seen a stage production of *Ibong Adarna* in high school, like most Filipino kids. So he had that memory to pull from as he watched from the third row of benches set up for an audience, with a view of the rink that allowed them to see over the boards.

Original music, original choreography, a shortened version of the story, with Filipino skaters and performers. When the rehearsal started and the ensemble took their places on the ice, he noticed that half of them seemed young, in their teens and pre-teens. A few were a little older, taller, rounder, but when the music started and they began to skate in sync, he sat up and paid attention.

And then he got overwhelmed.

This was too real.

Calinda was calling out beats and directions from the ice, a microphone attached to her cheek. When watched this way he could see that it wasn't perfect just yet. Someone wobbled, someone skated slightly off beat. But still, this was no casual hobby for any of the dozen or so people on the ice. Each little move was a fraction of what they dedicated years of their life to, hours of training, and all of their focus.

Too real. Before he realized it, before he could stop himself, he had pushed himself up and he was making his way down to the floor, and heading for the mall exit. He made it as far as the park, the same park they'd lingered at before the rink stop, and there he stopped to breathe. It was freaking hot, sometime past three p.m., and no one else was there. Safe enough then to go under the shade and try to collect himself, not knowing how far he'd scattered.

"Hey."

Naya's voice was gentle, and a polite distance away.

His glasses had fogged up from the rapid change in the surrounding climate, and he took them off. Wiping them on his shirt helped him not look directly at her, anyway. "Hey," he said, thankful that his voice didn't shake. "I'm heading back in. I just...I needed..."

"Needed what?"

"I don't know."

"You didn't like *Ibong Adarna*?"

"On the contrary. It looks like it'll be amazing. I mean, I can imagine with enough practice they'll soon catch up to their director's ambition. It just...overwhelmed me."

He wanted to explain why, but she wasn't asking. It was, actually, as if she already knew. "I'm going to hand you a bottle of water, okay? I'll need to come closer."

"I'm fine. Come as close as you want."

She smirked. "At least you're making jokes now." The bottle of water was a welcome coolness in his palm. "I'm going to touch your back, as a gesture of comfort, okay."

That she did—and holy hell it was comforting. He sagged toward her, without meaning to, but she was a stable shoulder and everything else to lean on and she let him lean.

"Water," she said. "Drink. And just a sec—I'm getting out of this sweater. Fuck, it's hot."

He was too close to see anything but a curtain of soft purple sweater swooshing past his face. This was the right time to drink water, like she ordered. He *was* feeling more composed; his breathing seemed to have gone back to normal.

"Calinda is milking a hobby," he said.

"What?"

"Calinda Valerio. That's what she's doing, isn't it? She loves what she does, and is unable to find opportunities to continue to do it, so she had to create them."

"It's a radical demotion of her commitment to the sport to call it a *hobby* but yeah—that's what she's doing. It's what she had to do, if she wanted to accomplish things."

See, he wasn't ready for that. Ben's career was from election to election, three-year or six-year intervals of life planning. It was becoming clearer and clearer to him that he was as in control of his *today* as a newbie on the ice.

"You don't have to figure it all out *today*, Ben," came her voice in his ear. "This is a moment. Don't pin everything you've got on this day. It's too much pressure."

"You say it'll get better?"

"You see anyone else here who has a better quitting story than me? No? Looks like you'll have to take my word for it."

9

As the van predictably crawled from Taguig to Pasay, Naya talked a little about the *Ibong Adarna* show. She was proud of this tour group today—after they watched the rehearsal they were able to get some Q&A time with Calinda and the skaters, and they were asking questions, noting schedules, asking if they could purchase tickets. And as well they should; Calinda was pouring her heart and soul into this, and while it wasn't going to replace the money and travel opportunities joining a international company would, it was at least a small step in that direction.

But if she wanted to make herself curl up into a ball and cry, all Naya needed to do was remind herself that *everything* seemed to be a baby step. So many people working so hard to take a freaking baby step. So many things were so difficult, and she wasn't sure if it was the world changing, or just that she got older and saw it for what it was. The idea that you could do that thing you love and change the world...did that really happen? Because if no one ever found out about it, then what world did it change? Naya thought of all the artists who stopped creating, just among those she knew of. All the well-meaning establishments, all the non-profits, all the tour concepts, travel-more campaigns...coming and going, whimpers in the greater noise of a world generally not caring about any of this.

And this is where you stop because you still need to get these people to the next place.

When small talk was over, she put her earphones in, huddled low in her van seat, and searched for Ben Cacho on YouTube. This wasn't out of line for her, even if other people found it strange. Years of her life were on video, online somewhere. Surely other people realized that it was the same for them? Even if the minutes or hours total varied, there was a professional or personal trail online and some of it would be so easy to find.

The top video was a speech he gave at a senior high school almost a year ago. Naya sank lower, making sure no one could see what she was watching, and pressed play. Applause, an empty podium, and then Ben walking up to it, adjusting the microphone. His blazer-shirt-tie combo was almost identical to what he had on that morning when she met him, but the circumstances were different, his demeanor was different. On this video he was owning each step, flashing a boyish charming smile as he fiddled with the equipment.

"Sorry about that," he said. *"I've gotten much taller since I was last here."*

Cute. Naya would have rolled her eyes if she weren't so falling-for-it.

"I was asked to come here to talk to you about what I do. My official position at work is speechwriter. But what I do, believe it or not, is learn history, and write history. Don't yawn, because this is not boring, and maybe you'll sit up straighter in class when

you realize that history is being made every day. Ms. Peregrino, you can thank me later. I've been asked to come over to tell all of you how I got my job, and in short, it takes a lot of work to be lucky.

"*I got my job because I needed one. I was in law school and for many reasons, I couldn't rely on my parents for money. But I didn't want to quit. My classmate was working off and on for then-congressman David Alano, who was going to speak at the opening of a new healthcare center. One day, my friend asked me to cover for him because he didn't know* how *to write a speech about a healthcare center.*

"*At the time, it didn't seem like my moment had arrived. I stepped up because I needed money, but I also had an idea of how to write this, which was more motivation than my friend had. Still, the idea came from the worst possible place, and that was losing my mother a few years before. I had so many thoughts and feelings about access to medication, women's health, early detection. I poured all of it into a draft—like I had written my heart and soul, and that got me noticed. That speech got edited to pieces, by the way, and the version David delivered only retained maybe fifteen percent of the original, but it was better, because it wasn't supposed to be about me. I was lucky, having an idea like that when the opportunity came along—but that's not what makes a good speechwriter all the time. When I joined their team, I didn't only draft speeches; I eventually edited the drafts of others. When I learned how to get a message across but not make it about me—*"

"Excuse me, Naya?"

Rochelle's presence behind her might not have been too sudden or too sneaky, but Naya was also rather shamefully stalking someone online so it was automatically too sudden. Her phone slipped from her fingers and fell to the floor, but thankfully screen-side down. "Yes, Rochelle?"

"I wasn't sure if I could get a few minutes with you, just the two of us," Rochelle said, "but I'm applying to colleges next year and I wonder if I could ask you for advice?"

"Ask Ben too," her mother said. "While we're here. We never get to see him."

"Mom, we can talk to Kuya Ben another time."

"Scoot over here, Naya, so we can talk to both of you. There's room in the back. I'm sure he'll have advice to share too."

So that was how Naya and Ben ended up on the back row of the van together, and how she confirmed that comforting soap-skin scent was his, and not from her clothes somehow, how she noticed the vibration of his knee as he tapped his foot while they talked. Was that a nervous habit? Was he nervous?

Based on earlier snippets of conversation, he was related to Mari and Rochelle, but they didn't have the closeness that family who at least saw each other regularly seemed to have. Rochelle was out here updating him on years of her life, and he definitely was as unaware of it as Naya was.

"...I just know I don't want law school," Rochelle was saying.

"It's breaking her dad's heart," Mari added. "Ben, tell her she shouldn't rule it out completely. Rochelle, Ben was so good in law school."

Naya saw him cringe, and maybe that was part of the problem. His poker face, also known as ruthless lawyer face, needed work. Or today was really not the day for him to have to do career counseling for an impressionable young person.

Shit, it wasn't the best day for her to do that either.

"I think it's about the kind of life you want to secure," Naya said, wondering if she was saving him properly. "You want to hit all the right notes, you know? Something you're good at so you can move up and grow, something you're interested in so you have an instinct for it that bored uninterested colleagues won't..."

"Something that will carry you through hard times, if life happens," Ben added.

"It's just that you seem to be so good at this, Naya," Rochelle said. "And I'm interested in all of these things. Sometimes I feel I like too many things? It's so much pressure to choose one career. And right now—I thought I'd be old enough to know by now."

Ben laughed and not without bitterness. "It always feels that way."

"If Rochelle wanted to be someone like you, Ben," Mari said, "what would she need to do?"

"Like me how?"

"A speechwriter," Naya reminded him.

"She can write," Mari said of her daughter. "She's been asked to edit her classmates' speeches before."

Rochelle rolled her eyes. "Fixing a presentation for an English report is different, Mom."

"Still. When else can we ask Kuya Ben how to do it?"

"You learn as much as you can," Ben said. "You get familiar with research. Fact checking. Giving sources proper credit. Knowing where to find them, even. And then, composing your argument in a compelling way."

"I don't like debate," Rochelle said.

"It's not debate, not all the time. It's a *position*. Something needs to be done, or defended, or upheld."

"She can learn to do that," Mari shrugged. "If she puts her mind to it."

"Then she has to look for opportunities to practice.

Intern for people she eventually wants to write for. Get the chance to work for the people who do the writing."

"You trained under Elmo Laranas. He's a legend among media practitioners."

Ben winced, Naya saw it clear as day. "I worked *with* Elmo when he was heading the campaign, and when he became chief of staff. All the writers were trained by Tana Cortes."

"Oh, I'm not familiar with that name."

"She was an outside consultant. She didn't...she didn't join the staff when David got elected."

"So what you're saying is find someone to apprentice with, like Elmo Laranas?"

"No," Ben said, trying to keep his voice level. "I guess I'd say try to find someone like Tana Cortes."

"That's years of work, right?" Rochelle was not feeling this.

"It'll always be," Naya said. "For anything."

"But it's years of work for someone you might not like," Rochelle said. "Someone who might have done shady things. Someone who might be using your words to cover up the shady things."

Ben laughed and tried to smother it in his wrist. "Tita Mari, your daughter has principles. Don't send her off to politics."

"Your boss has principles," Mari retorted. "I campaigned for David Alano among all my friends."

"He does have them, though," he relented.

"I campaigned for him because he's at least trying to turn certain things around. It's scary, what we're allowing the future to become for Rochelle, for our kids. That means we should be helping these people, encouraging them, right? Because a broken system just needs those willing to fix it."

"Maybe," Rochelle said, "I want to do all of that but not really how Kuya Ben's done it. I mean look at Naya—she's taught me so much."

Wow. Naya pressed her lips together, but then all eyes were on her like they were expecting her to say something. "Career paths are a personal thing," she said diplomatically, she hoped. "I'm doing this because I can. At some point if people change their minds, to protect themselves or, you know, just so they can live with themselves, that's fine too."

"I want to know what *Naya* studied," Rochelle sort-of whined.

"Media and film," Naya told her. "Back then I did it because it seemed fun, to watch movies and be graded on that, but later it made sense to me because I was studying platforms. I was studying how to use an evolving thing."

"That requires a personality that can adapt," Ben said.

"I guess I am that, so it worked."

"But how do you know you can adapt?" he continued. "How do you find out, as someone Rochelle's age, that you can study a platform because you already have the temperament and skill for it? How does it feel like that, instead of feeling like you're fucking up most of the time?"

Naya blinked. "Language, Ben."

Rochelle giggled. "It's fine, Naya. And it's a legit question."

She didn't know how to answer it. She was also very close to offering to add liquor to their dinner, but she wasn't going to say that to the seventeen-year-old in front of her mother.

Maybe she would offer it privately to Ben instead.

10

P asay, 5:50 p.m.

SO NOW HE was wondering where Naya had been, all his life.

They went to different universities. She worked while he was in law school. They were never introduced. Had no common friends. Really? No one, out of everyone in their age bracket, who worked in similar projects? Not a true friend among them all. He almost—maybe for real—wished he had known her longer, because no one else made sense of what had happened to him the same way that she did.

Not that she sugarcoated anything. Things still sucked. But he...trusted her? She didn't have an angle.

That wasn't completely right; she had an angle, but it wasn't a problem for him. Did not interfere with his. That was part of his job, to keep track of past angles and predict future ones. Exhausting as fuck, but it was his default setting.

Not anymore. Doesn't have to be.

He liked learning, right? He said as much at least once today, this odd day. So he should be paying attention to the mini lecture happening now as they stood at the driveway of the Catala, the hotel that was apparently their last stop for the day. Naya was explaining the work that went into the restoration of the buildings that formed the compound that comprised this hotel. Something about the value of preserving the art we use. Instead, that was only the sound-track to watching her against the backdrop of a beautiful building and a purple then orange sky. At some point, she'd lost the ponytail and her hair was free, dark brown, and down past her shoulders. When he felt he shouldn't be looking at her like that, he looked down. He saw her sneak-ers, saw how she pointed her foot, how she turned her body by the hip when describing their location.

Ben stepped back, tried to put more distance between him and Naya, which didn't make sense because she was all the way over there anyway, and he was already lingering at the fringe of the group. That step brought him slightly closer to a conversation already happening.

"...really looking forward to this. I mean lunch was awesome, but I've been meaning to try the food here." That was Danny, the guy traveling with Dexter from the ad agency, and Jana, the lady traveling with the other guy.

"I have," Jana said. "The lamb's excellent. And the drink with the little jellies."

"Have you tried the food here, Ben?"

Ben was not expecting to be spoken to, but the gears shifted and he cleared his throat. "No, no I haven't. I didn't even know this place was already open."

For someone who had never spoken to Ben before that moment, Danny was great at just going with it. Ben admired that in people, envied it sometimes. "I've been bugging Dexter for the longest time. Well, not so long—the hotel's been open maybe less than a year. But yeah. I can't stand his work hours, and I could've gone with other friends already, but I wanted to go here with him first, you know?"

"You're here now," Ben said, "but also with a tour group."

"Oh," Danny waved a hand dismissively. "I like people. This is fine."

"You work for the government?" Jana asked, but it was the polite and somewhat detached tone of someone who didn't live in the country and probably had little idea what that could mean.

"I used to," Ben said. "Speechwriter. When did you move to Manila?"

"Ten months ago. It's a secondment, but they haven't told me yet what the next assignment is so I want to go on these tours as much as I can."

"What do you do?"

"Finance." Jana laughed. "It's not so interesting to talk about."

"I work in construction," Danny said. "So don't tell me about boring. But it doesn't have to be; there's a story everywhere. Being at a hotel like this can get me all geeky. I heard nice things about the tiles they used."

"I'd rather talk about tiles than my job," Ben admitted.

"Danny, Jana," Naya called. "We can head inside now." She eyed him like she was wondering what he had done or said to them, and he held his hands up because he had nothing.

∾

LATER, and as a pleasant surprise, his hand then held a cold bottle of craft beer and it was Naya who put it there. It wasn't part of the prepped dinner for the tour but dinner was over, and they were encouraged to look around and see as much as they could of the Catala before Naya sent them off.

Ben didn't feel like going around. Instead he stepped out onto the balcony of the second-floor restaurant, following the tile pattern all the way to the railing. The tiles *were* pretty, not that he ever thought about it before. It was nice that people cared enough about the things that some people would never notice.

Naya followed him out, and gave him the beer. He could see the courtyard pool, a gazebo, several benches, a small garden. Dexter and Danny were down there, but the others were in the building still.

"So this is what your day looks like," Ben said.

She smiled at him, letting out a breath, allowing herself to deflate a little. "The places change, but yeah, if by dinner I'm at a nice place with great food, that's a good day."

"You do that for people, too."

"What?"

"You give people a day like that. You give them a good day."

Naya tipped her bottle and drank. "I guess I do. It's not a bad gig."

"You're amazing."

"Am I."

"You know I'm not shitting you."

"You write spin for a living."

"I'd debate you on that, but you know I'm not overstating. I'm not lying. I'm not even mildly exaggerating. You are amazing."

"Oh. You are too, Ben."

"You don't have to return the compliment."

"Yeah, maybe learn to recognize a truth when it's being said to you too, mister. I think you've had a rough day, but it'll get better."

The sound that came out of Ben was almost laughter. "Do you promise?"

"Yes, I promise."

So many lights around him. Stars behind her. Garden lights. The dancing bright circles reflecting off the pool. And something in her eyes.

"This happens," she said, softly. The eyes were closer, because she had stepped closer. "It happens to travelers. You're thrown together on a trip, or a tour, and it's a confined space for hours at a time. You reveal interesting things about each other. It's all exciting and new and it's not exactly the real world. Do you know what I'm talking about?"

"I think I do."

"It happens. You bond during a tour and become best friends, become more than that, you think you've met the best person by chance in the strangest place, you promise to keep in touch. And you don't, but that's okay. It happens."

Then her eyes were closer, because he had stepped closer.

He knew what she was saying. Maybe another day he'd ask for her stories, her twenty-four-hour best buddies, if she'd had beach trip hookups, eight-hour soulmates. But he didn't, because Ben still knew a thing or two about words. Sometimes he *could* make it about himself.

"Is that a bad thing?" Ben asked her. "Everything you just said."

"I don't hook up while I'm working," Naya said.

He took a gulp and the bitter, sweet, nutty, fruity brew rolled down his throat. "What time is it?"

There was a clock somewhere on the wall behind him, he assumed, because she tilted her head and then smirked. "Eight p.m."

"How long is your work day, really?"

Her eyes twinkled he was damn sure of it. "Look at that, I'm off the clock."

"That's great."

"It is."

"What do you mean by—"

The next half step was hers; her lips claimed his. Soft lips, pushing, opening, taking his lips, his mouth. He pushed back, kissed back.

"Yes! Oh my God, yes!" Commotion downstairs had them break their kiss. Naya pressed a finger to the corner of her mouth, but she was unconcerned.

"Dexter proposed to Danny," she explained. "He wanted to do that tonight, here."

"You helped them do that."

"I guess I did." Naya looked at the clock again. "I need to officially close the tour and make sure everyone gets their rides home. Do you want to hang around here with me after?"

"Of course." To Ben the answer was obvious. What else was he going to do?

aya, this is a test.

An intelligent, attractive man. Someone you seem to be able to stand, even on his worst day.

A free hotel room.

What do you do?

The first real heartbreak of Naya's life happened in the "real world," after an intense six days on a solo backpacking trip to Bohol and Siquijor. Solo because she set out from Manila on her own. This was not her first go at multi-city backpacking, at island hopping, at developing feelings for the guy she met at the beach who said all the right things. Not even the first time she considered and then did sleep with someone on the first date. She thought she had found and donned the armor needed by a modern woman negotiating life through temporary relationships. But *that* heartbreak, when it all fell apart once they returned to life in the city, also reminded her that she could get things so fucking wrong.

Not that it ruined her. It did ruin trip romances somewhat. Naya was someone else when she was on the road, and other people were too—forcing that into the "real world" never worked out.

So the armor got an upgrade: Enjoy the trip flirt, the trip fling, the trip fuck...but don't expect it to write. Or call. Or acknowledge you on social media. Or be anything that could be transplanted to another place and remain exactly as it was.

If she suggested *her* place as the next location for her and Ben...wrong answer. She was in between leases and living with her parents. Besides, they may have met in their home city but this definitely had the makings of a trip fling. Trip fling *extreme*, because lord, perhaps someone shouldn't be as upfront about his vulnerability to a stranger. She could do harm with all that information.

It didn't matter what the right answer was; she cashed in a perk from her "income-generating hobby" and got them into a free room at that very hotel.

"This is beautiful," Ben said, the natural reaction so far to walking into any standard room at the Catala. The design and styling of all the rooms were impeccable, but she did say that in a lecture earlier that night. Maybe he wasn't paying attention.

Beautiful room. Two walls of windows, gauzy curtains and heavy drapes keeping them from being seen by the rest of the city. King-size bed, looking nice and poofy-comfy. Identical orange lamps on either side had switched on as they came in, throwing spheres of warm light. Flattering warm light.

"So," he said, apparently after surveying the space. "Walk me through this."

"You're a virgin?"

"No." A confused-amused little smile came to his face. "I meant the travel hookup."

"Oh." *Naya, think about why your heart skipped a little. But later.*

He was probably thinking about it *now.* "What did you want me to be?"

She laughed. "Exactly who you are and no one else. Please continue."

"We're travelers. We spent a day exploring some city. We get a room. What happens next?"

Naya set her backpack down on the wooden desk next to her. "You take note of the exits. Did you?" `

That probably wasn't what he thought he would hear. "Uh, yes."

"You take a good long moment and assess how you feel, physically. I gave you a drink earlier. How much of it did you have?"

"Not a lot."

"Do you feel dizzy? Nauseous? Less inhibited?"

Ben's Adam's apple moved; the rest of his body was still. "I feel less inhibited, but I won't attribute it to my drink being compromised."

"Put your belongings where they'll always be in your line of sight."

He had a heavy backpack with him and he set it down on the low bench at the foot of the bed. "Got it."

"Understand that coming into the room doesn't have to mean it goes all the way between us. You, or I, can call an end to this and take the exit. You can do that now, or at any point."

He nodded, so obediently.

"Ben," Naya said. "If you already know this, I can stop. I probably sound patronizing. We're both old enough to know all of this, right?"

"I know. I mean, it's not top-of-mind info, but I get it. I...I like hearing you give a lecture."

Oh God. Naya wanted to laugh. She would have, if she weren't suddenly so turned on. "You're unbelievable."

"And you're amazing. Does that make us even?"

"Do you have condoms?"

"I don't."

"I do. Next time don't get in a situation where you have to rely on someone else doing the responsible thing. They could be lying about everything else."

He looked properly chastened. "I have some at home. I would have answered this differently if we were at my place."

But she *wouldn't* have gone to his place. She hadn't explained that rule yet, but she was going to keep this to herself for now.

"Do we talk about dating status?" Ben asked. "I'm single."

"Me too," Naya replied.

"But—yeah, we could be lying. I see."

"The upside of the travel fling," Naya added, "is that you can start over with someone else. Of course you do it as smart as you can, and you draw those lines you don't cross."

"Lines like?"

"I don't lead someone on, if they're not on the same page. Like if they're thinking it'll be more than what it is. I don't cheat, or help people cheat."

"How can you know that though?"

"You ask them, but you don't trust their answer. It's how they answer, really. Also, you look them up."

"Okay, makes sense."

"All of this, it doesn't have to be a permanent shift. When I'm traveling, I'm already starting over. My job, my errands, everything is so far away. The connection I make with someone can stay right where it is. It can be whatever I need it to be."

"Is that a good thing? That it won't last?"

Naya reached into her backpack for the pouch that carried her condom stash. Yes, she had it. Yes, it had more than one, not that carrying more than one meant anything. Only that she was as prepared as she told other people to be.

"Ask yourself first what you need this to be, Ben. You don't have to say it out loud. I don't need to hear it."

It didn't get this *technical*, this step-by-step on the other times that she got to this point. This part would have happened at dinner, at drinks, in the moment before she decided to get in the elevator with some guy, cross the doorway into a bedroom. But this guy liked instructions, liked her words, so she stood there and thought about what she needed from him, and he probably did the same.

He pulled his blazer off, one arm at a time, and dropped it on the bed. "All right," he said. "I've thought of what I need. You?"

She nodded. "Yeah."

"Then?"

"Come here and show me."

∾

SO THIS WAS what she got, when she challenged him to show her what he wanted: His hands on her body. Palms cupping around parts of her that curved. He pulled her clothing tight and splayed his fingers like he was using them to measure her shoulder, her neck, collarbones. He could cover an entire breast with his open hand. Her nipples felt his caress and hardened, almost to the point of pain.

"You're a hands guy," she said, suddenly breathless.

"Always," he said. Those hands curved around her waist, her hips, then pulled her to him, ground her into his hardness. "I like how you feel."

"I...feel *you*." Ugh, stating the obvious. She felt him twitch against her, or that was her pressing closer onto him, her jeans and his pants so many layers but also so much friction. They hadn't even kissed yet, again. She told herself it didn't need to go so far, maybe she'd be content making out until she needed water, then she'd kick him out, and enjoy her staycation in peace. Tell that to Naya five minutes into the future, one leg wrapped around this guy like he was a tree and she was about to freaking climb.

Naya was a quick decision maker, sometimes.

Climb it is.

He took his shirt off and hello, familiar body from this morning. Hello, body she'd *observed* earlier, nice to meet you again. Now she had permission to take a long hard look. She had permission to touch.

She had permission to taste.

He caught her mouth in his before she could try anything. She had barely done anything, and he made a move again; she should have told him she preferred the rhythm of her, then him, then her, then him. Travel flings, while exciting in theory, were also a scary first few minutes of realizing this man knew nothing about you. That he might take what he wanted before you got yours.

"May I," Ben said. She felt his hands on her shirt and when she nodded, he pulled it over her head. Fingers hooked around her bra straps and they were free, bra unhooked and tossed somewhere a moment later.

"I want to see you come, right now," Ben said. "What's the fastest way?"

Me then him, then me, then him, the rhythm was all messed up. It felt like *me me me* but Naya wasn't going to correct him. She unbuttoned her jeans and dropped them, kicked them away, lifted a leg to open herself up. She wasn't sure anymore if she managed to give the instruction because the feeling of his finger slipping under her panties, touching her where she throbbed, was the right answer. God, was it the right answer.

"So hot," he groaned. "So wet."

Well yeah, Captain Obvious. Naya gasped when he increased the pressure, licked a wide swath on his neck when he pushed a finger inside, and then two.

"I want you to come," he said. "How do you want to do it?"

"Faster. Like that. Just—fast."

It wasn't *so* fast. It was, still, long minutes of her hanging on, guiding his hand, delicious hard thrusting, and then *there*, her control snapping away from her.

She might have screamed. It was likely.

She collapsed and he caught her.

12

So, Ben. What kind of day has it been?

He expected to tell himself today, and days after, that it could have been worse. The day that marked his exit from his government job could have been much, much more humiliating. Much, much more demoralizing. Much, much more terrifying. That was just the way of the world now. Instead...

Instead it was still the same day, and yet at this moment he was rolling a condom over his hard, so hard, so painfully hard dick and pushing it into her. This brand of condom Naya carried was better than his usual, or maybe it was not having done this in a while, but he felt welcomed, hugged by her tight warmth.

It was kind of intense.

She gave him a pass to walk away at any point but damn, this day. He wouldn't ever be described as the impulsive type but he did like to see things through.

Yes, that was his excuse.

He didn't *want* to move. He was all the way inside her and he wanted to stay like that for as long as he could.

"Fuck," he said.

"Yeah, get on that."

How to, without coming within a second? "Gimme a sec," Ben pleaded. Then—then he began counting presidents. And years in office. In order. He did *not* mean to do that—told himself never to do that again—but he needed to focus and it just happened.

He withdrew slowly and plunged back inside her...and he did it. He could do it again. His will was back, it was stronger, he might get through this without ruining it for both of them.

However, it turned out he at least would get to have this memory, and know that Naya was worth it. He loved the sounds she made, how her lips felt on his skin, how her fingers touched him. Taken together it was all the signs of want, of wanting, of needing, of relief at getting. He wanted to be right about how he read this. Whenever he pushed into her, he wanted more; he took her tongue in his mouth and wanted it again and again.

Taking all of the cues again, she seemed to have liked it even more when he took her from behind. The moans were louder, more urgent. She was holding her breasts, squeezing them, and he took over that and filled his hands with soft curves. She came once this way, dropped her forehead to the bed, falling to the mattress because the pillow was somewhere else, and let out a low scream. He felt her come, felt her pulsing around him.

Ben got through that. Not that he congratulated himself because then Naya shifted positions, got on her back, and told him just how she wanted him to take her. Standing up, she said, driving into her as she looked up at him from the bed.

He could barely touch her, in this position. He was

holding on to her thighs, but touching wasn't the point. The point was *watching*, and it was overwhelming, seeing how her body quivered with each thrust. And she was watching him, how tight his torso had gotten, how his face focused on this one thing, because he stopped thinking about pace and lasting and just wanted to fuck. Her. Them. He came hard. It was a new record, not that he had a way of stack ranking them. But this was hard, and he felt spent, boneless, obliterated.

Also he felt like he was on top of the world.

What a day.

～

BEN WASN'T REALLY *OBLITERATED* by the sex. He liked using those words sometimes. Truth was, seconds after coming, his good sense came back and he eased out of her to check if the condom caught everything. It did.

Great, in terms of things actually working.

By the time he came back from throwing the used condom and washing himself, Naya had crawled up to the middle of the bed and wrapped a sheet around her. "Hey," she said.

He was naked, and felt it. She probably wouldn't mind if he started dressing up, so he picked up his pants and boxers and started at it. "That might have turned my day around."

She laughed. "Yes, that definitely did not suck."

Naya was smiling, but she was letting her gaze go around the room, and she wasn't telling him to keep his clothes off. Ben didn't have to have that translated for him.

"What's proper etiquette post-travel hookup?" he said.

"All we have to do is agree that we're not obligated to contact each other after. Or do this again." Naya hugged the blanket around herself. "Some people do meet the love of their life traveling, but most will not. Or they could have something at the moment but it's a bubble, and it won't be the same even if they try to make it work. Their real lives are just so..."

"Unstable?"

"...different."

Of course. Never mind if this was the best sex he'd had in years; he was still going to wake up tomorrow without a job. Possibly with bridges burned across different places where he could work. He might not have a reputation to hang on to; they might have ruined even that by the time the sun came up again.

"That's fair," Ben said. "I had...I had a great day, Naya. I can't even believe the day I had."

Naya pulled herself up to her knees, blanket wrapped around her, and made her way closer to him. He was at the right angle to kiss her, so he did, and she kissed him back nice and lazy and slow. "You don't suck, Ben. Good night."

He couldn't feel bad about that.

13

F*ive months later*

MELLY: *Are you going to reply?*

It took Naya a full second to register that the message came from Melly, and not the depths of her subconscious showing up as a text on her phone.

Naya: *Of course.*

She and Ben had *not* kept in touch since he showed up in her van and then...walked out of her hotel room. Part of the arrangement, and even though there were ways to find him, she didn't. Some nights were rough, she had to admit. Like that date her mom got her into, and it was not fun at all, and Naya was looking at her watch at eleven p.m. and telling herself if she knew where Ben was, she could still save that day.

But that was wrong.

Anyway. A message she got on her tour promo page that morning, but sent at three a.m.:

Naya, sorry this is short notice but can we meet tomorrow? Or today, because you'll probably see this in the morning. Tell me where. Breakfast, or as early as you can. Thank you.

(It's for work.)

Hello, good morning. :)

The page's messages could be seen by Melly too, even if their "income-generating hobby" partnership had come to an end. Which Naya insisted was totally okay, and Melly normally didn't come back in with opinions about what she was doing, until right now.

Melly: *Contacting you for work wink wink*

Naya: *I'm a real-life communications consultant with media training DUH.*

Melly: *You also real-life travel flung him heehee*

Naya: *You know my thing about that*

Melly: *I'm not judging, I am totally shipping. And you crossed your own line when you travel flung a guy who lives in Manila DUH.*

Naya: *Travel flung is not a word*

Melly: *That's what you DID. Is it so bad that he wants to see you again and maybe not just for work?*

Naya: *It doesn't work out when you meet outside your regular life like that. I know.*

Melly: *But every day of your life is like that who else are you going to meet and what else will be a regular life for you both???*

Naya: *Stop that*

Melly: *I love you and want you to have a good day every day*

Naya: *That can't happen*

Melly: *But you make it happen for people every time*

Naya: *These things end and I don't have patience for the recovery time required, babe*

Melly: *Boo hoo*

Naya: *Boo hoo you. What are you doing checking the page? We're not partners anymore.*

Melly: *I do still check it. You might need me.*

Naya did, because Melly not being available anymore meant Naya had to hire a driver, and get a van that wasn't as nice when she needed to tour, and that ate into either the experience or what she earned. Because she didn't want the experience to erode, she earned less instead. But Melly had been extremely supportive already for as long as she could, agreeing to earning percentages instead of charging per day she helped out. Then her deadline came and she went back to work, teaching college-level marketing and working on her MBA.

Naya was happy for her cousin, swear to God. Melly was also her landlord now, of sorts, so she had no right to be snippy.

Naya: *Right. Get your chismis elsewhere today.*

Melly: *If I didn't leave so early I'd hang out with you both haha. Tell me everything ha!!!*

Breakfast, or as early as possible, Ben had asked. Naya had a schedule, an entire day planned without him. There was that thing she had been putting off forever, that she was sort of maybe going to do finally...

She had a life, damn it, and there were rules to getting back in touch with the travel fling. Was she the kind of girl who got sent messages at three a.m. and then showed up at breakfast hours later?

Naya told Ben she'd meet him at ten-thirty.

～

HE LOOKED...LIKE Ben on the day she met him. Round neck

shirt underneath a buttoned charcoal blazer. Dark jeans. Glasses on, hair still wet from a recent shower. She asked him to meet her at the park at Six 32 Central, because they could buy takeout coffee and talk there. Outdoor, conveniently near her next appointment, and it didn't have to *mean anything*.

She wouldn't have looked exactly the same. Today was Serious Errand Day, and she had to look the part. Brown trousers, white lace top, belt that looked like a scarf. Embroidered flats, instead of her usual sneakers. Not enough time to get her hair done, but it was cooperating after a spritz of hair mist, so that would do.

He was already waiting, sitting on one of the benches when she showed up. Maybe he didn't expect seeing her cleaned up, but something changed in his face. He kind of looked floored. Naya was not sure how to feel about that.

"Naya."

"Ben."

Started with a handshake, an awkward touch then half a jiggle, then they both kind of pressed forward and then it was a little hug. She told herself she'd be cool, when she saw him again. She was very cool, for sure. Naya was also hoping for another round. Girl needed her good sex, though not exactly that moment.

"Thank you for meeting me," he said. "And I moved to a place near here so it was a nice walk. Do you live nearby too?"

"Oh, no. But I'm supposed to be in the area for a thing anyway."

A pause, and then a lot of breathing of faintly-floral scented air.

"It's so good to see you, Naya."

"You shouldn't be emailing people at three a.m."

"Are you kidding me? Only true friends do that. Trusted confidantes. You're in my circle of trust, is what that means."

"What do you need?"

"Let's sit down?" He offered the bench and they sat there together. "So I do need something from you today, but I did want to get in touch before now. For the record."

"For the record, I did too."

"I had a great time. That one and only time."

"Hmm." *So unfortunate. Maybe we should schedule something.* But Naya remained cool, remembered herself.

"And you don't know how many times I wanted to call you, to meet up because I wanted to ask you about things. Like actual career things. But I didn't know if you wanted that. I didn't want the next time I saw you to be you consoling me again over drinks about my unemployment. There was a lot of that the past few months."

"Are you okay, Ben?" It didn't sound so horrible though, the idea of going out for a drink, talking about work. Or lack thereof.

"Yes, I am. It took a while, but I'm getting there."

"You look okay," Naya said, sincere as hell. She *had* been more than a little worried about him, at first when she was reading news about his resignation, and then more when the news cycle moved on. His name on the news was a quick blip—not even enough to make him a household name. That also meant she stopped getting updates about him and he dropped out of her life as suddenly as how he had come in.

"Thank you. It got rough for a bit. I mean, you saw how it started."

Ben didn't just look okay. He looked *energized*. A bit tired, but put together. This was way closer to the guy she saw giving a speech to high school students, charming and intelligent, ready with something to say.

"How are you, Naya?"

She was starting to feel like her trousers were too much and her top was too lacy. "Same. I mean, I have things to do today, but that's not for several hours."

"Still doing tours, right? I mean, you answered the message I sent on your page."

"I am. But by myself now, because Melly's gone off to do her thing."

"Is that harder?"

"Kind of." It was slightly overcast, which was a good thing because it wasn't too hot, and she could stay out there with him and maintain her composure somewhat. Composure she'd lose for sure if she opened up about the work troubles *now*. "What do you need?" she said again. What else could he need from her? He seemed to have gotten his life back on track just fine on his own.

Ben's smile was mischievous, a little sneaky, and completely cute. "Your tour guide powers."

"Today? Right now?"

"Today, Naya. It's that kind of day. Will you help me?"

14

Ben had wanted to call Naya the next day, honest truth.

However, he had a talk with himself and accepted that it wasn't the right time. First, moping. Then, getting his life back on track. He resolved to only meet up with her again when he was in a better place, and he wasn't exactly there yet, but he needed her anyway, so what was the harm in skipping over a few things.

Today he was being ambitious. Maybe he'd volunteered to do too much. He only knew that Naya would help him and she wouldn't stab him in the back. Which should have given him pause about his course of action, but anyway.

"I can't do that," Naya said, surprising him, after he told her "the plan."

He was up late, had little sleep, and maybe it wasn't the best plan—but the way she was reacting, maybe asking her to get her friends to leak David Alano's hotel room number at the Carter Pacific was over the top.

"Why not?" he asked. "Can't your friends do that?"

"It's unethical to give out that kind of information, or put my friends in that position," she said, like it was the most natural thing in the world. "That's why you came to find me? To get my friends *fired*?"

"Well *no*. Of course we're not doing anything unethical." But now Naya's arms were crossed and she was giving him a stern look. "I was speculating on what was possible, given your connections in the hotel industry. *Of course* I'm not asking you to violate anyone's privacy. *Of course.*"

"Why can't you just text him? Like how *people* do it. You have his number, don't you? Ask him what his room number is, maybe he'll actually tell you."

Yes, that would actually make sense, wouldn't it? Ben had only recently returned to the fringes of political life and already he was being reminded how absurd it was on a daily basis. Maybe Naya had forgotten; it *had* been a while for her. "He has a work phone and work social media profiles and I never know who is looking at it at any given time. The other person who has access to it is exactly the person who shouldn't see it."

"You can't talk to him anywhere else?" Naya was chewing her lip now. "Seems like it would be easier to 'run into' him at a public event."

He thought of this, but when he managed to ask a former colleague about David's schedule, it didn't look like the he would be able to sneak in. Ben wasn't welcome at the Senator's office, not right now. It would raise too many questions, and he didn't want his presence to be a red flag. Not that he was any good at being "on the field"—but he was working now, and he volunteered, and he wanted to do well.

And maybe he thought he could always ask Naya for help.

Ben started working again a month ago. One month, almost to the day, when he finally got to use that card.

I don't know how to do that. I'll ask Naya for help.

So here they were. "I already checked—he'll be at work all day until he heads out for dinner and then the hotel."

"And you can't show up at the office."

"No, that's probably going to make things worse."

"You're sure the hotel will be the Carter Pacific?"

"I know for sure it's the Carter Pacific. He's delivering a keynote early in the morning at a conference there, and it's too far from where he lives; he usually books a room the night before."

"Is he with people when he's at the hotel?"

"He'll be with the guy—with Elmo—all day. He'll probably be having drinks with him at the hotel right before he goes up to his room. It's a thing they do."

"Ben."

"Yes?"

"Is this shady stuff?"

"It *looks* like it? But I assure you it's not that bad."

"It's politics."

"Okay, so it's sort of shady. But it's me. Would you believe me if I said I'm trying to do the right thing here?"

"What exactly are you doing?"

"Delivering a message. Making sure he gets to talk to someone tonight."

She looked out toward the mall beyond the park, maybe thinking of a solution to his problem, maybe forming the right words to send him away. He hoped it wasn't the latter. "Ben, admit it."

Words clogged his throat. *What?* he thought, but didn't say.

"You were up for an adventure today, weren't you?"

He felt a surge of relief from not being dismissed yet. *An adventure.* He wouldn't have said that. That was a Naya phrase, because she probably used that and applied it to life. See, that was why he wanted her back already. Any kind of framing of this scary life change to an adventure was going to be helpful, would keep him from backing out.

"I know the Carter Pacific," Naya said. "The front desk isn't at the lobby. There's a café instead, and two lounges up at the front desk floor. You'll have various interception points and probably won't cause a scene, if you find him at the right time, and there's no need to find out what his room number is. How long do you need to speak to him?"

"If he's okay with it? Just a few minutes, really."

She nodded, starting to chew at her bottom lip. "You think he'll be driving himself up to the hotel?"

"No, he won't be."

"And this Elmo guy will be attached to him until he takes off for his room?"

"Most likely."

"I can probably help you, but I have *stuff* to do. It's still errand day for me, you know."

"Of course," Ben said. "I have a car and can take you anywhere you need to go."

"Don't you have other things to scheme?"

"You're part of the scheme, and we start tonight anyway. Let me help you do errand day."

"It's just—"

"Where are the errands?"

"A bunch of places."

"I don't mind, I really don't. I won't ask what we're doing there."

"I appreciate that."

"Unless you want to talk about it. And then on to the scheme. You'll help me? I'll drive you?"

He wasn't sure if he addressed all of her concerns, but

her look of hesitation disappeared. "It's hard to turn down an offer to drive me anywhere, especially during horrid errand day. Yes, Ben. Thank you."

"Awesome. We'll have an adventure."

"I don't know if you're using it right," Naya said. "It's not that kind of day."

For him it was, already. He'd tell her all about it later.

15

The first stop on this unfortunate See This Naya "adulting" tour was a clinic three blocks down from the park. She didn't even think about it, but as the sign flashed at her she realized that she maybe should have left Ben at the park and then met him after this thing. She didn't need a ride. But when she checked the time and said her appointment was soon, and started walking, he fell into step beside her and she let him.

"So it's this kind of errand," she said, pausing before she pulled the glass door to let them both in. "I shouldn't take too long. This place is pretty efficient; it's why I choose it when I have to. Do you want to wait at a coffee shop somewhere first?"

"I saw one across the street, yeah."

Naya did too. Across the street was the right amount of distance, if she wanted that, and he was sharp enough to suggest it. But then, she didn't want the distance? She was happy to see him. "You know, it really won't take that long. Save your cup of coffee for later. Just wait for me here?"

What? So she managed to surprise herself with that one.

That wasn't too clingy, was it? *You were ready to do this alone today. What's up, girl?*

Thankfully, Ben did not act as skeptical as her own inner monologue. In fact, he slid into the pause and pulled the door open for both of them. "This is reminding me of stuff I need to get done."

And it just reminded her that he lost his mom to sickness and it affected him enough to write a passionate speech about it. Was she the worst? She was the worst. "I'm sorry. When...was the last time you did your labs?"

"Two years ago? I did the executive annual physical for the first time and...it was a lot. Makes you think about your life. I've been 'too busy' for it for a while."

As a matter of fact she *was* doing that, thinking about her life choices, even before she got the message that he wanted to meet. Naya was used to having her sugar, uric acid, all these values checked yearly. She even calibrated her diet when something was on the high side. Not something she thought about when she was younger and had a regular job, but when she left corporate, reality bit—she couldn't take her health for granted. Sometimes she lost a day's income because of Manila's weather, but she got it back as soon as the sun reappeared. When she got sick, it was hard to function, even when her temperature was back to normal. She needed to be a hundred percent all the time, otherwise people wouldn't want to pay for the pleasure of being shown around.

She wasn't ready to admit it to anyone who knew her back then, but those days of traveling all day, editing for hours, and having a video up the same day or first thing the next morning? Naya could not do that anymore. She didn't even want to.

Lately she was doing this a lot. Second-guessing herself,

the choices that led her to this. But Ben did not know her then, so it was okay to show *some* cracks in the armor. "It's a pain but we have to do it."

He shrugged. "We're not immortal. Are you afraid of needles?"

"I'm not. This shouldn't take too long. I'll be back in a sec."

The way the clinic was laid out, Ben could sit in the waiting room and not have to see her get her blood drawn. He didn't have to see her head to a small bathroom with a cup, then go out and hand it half-full of pee to the nurse. That would have been too much, for a second day ever with someone.

Fifteen minutes later she emerged back out into the waiting room, hands clean, and nodded toward the door. "Done."

He'd been reading something on his phone—he did not do that the whole time on her tour, and it was funny to see him do a normal thing. This time he was quick to put the phone in his pocket and out of sight again once she showed up. "Awesome. Where's the next stop?"

"One of the portals to hell," she answered. "Or not, if we're lucky."

~

THEY WERE ONLY in the car for thirty minutes maximum, but she liked how he drove. Smooth, sure of himself. She watched how his hand rested on the gear stick in the moments before he tensed his muscles and used it. She liked being on a passenger seat, watching someone drive, looking at their profile. Noticed his strong jaw, his eyelashes, the way the world changed slightly through the filter of his eyeglasses. A few times he'd glance at her and she would avert her eyes somewhere else, forward, but this was a good view. No regrets.

The second stop was the nearest NBI Clearance office, still within the neighborhood but Ben didn't want to have to walk back all that way to pick up his car.

"NBI," Ben said, when he saw where they were headed. "Dear God."

Naya hadn't ordered and picked up an NBI Clearance in years, but reviews online said this branch was not so hellish, all things considered.

"I'll wait outside for you," he added.

"Avoiding the NBI, Ben?"

"Makes me itchy. I'll be here when you're done."

It didn't make sense for him to go inside with her anyway. One didn't "hang out" in government agencies for the fun of it—they were places that sucked you in for hours just because. Although the printout in Naya's bag assured her that she had an appointment.

It took less than half an hour to be done with lining up, and biometrics, and waiting for the actual clearance. Ben wasn't right outside the door though, but she eventually found him having coffee at the Starbucks on the ground floor.

"Done?" he asked.

"Yep." Naya took a seat at the same table and looked at the printout for a second, wondering if she should have her second coffee of the day. "Don't rush your drink—my next appointment isn't for a few more hours. And I need strength for it."

"So you're cleared?"

"By the NBI? Yes, always."

"Good for you."

"My name is Amansinaya Nicoletta Llamas," she said. "That's why I'm always clear. Thanks, Mom and Dad, for a name some kids made fun of when I was young, but gets me through every time now because no one with the same name has committed a crime."

"Old fashioned justice. I'm so impressed. *Amansinaya*."

"I know, right."

"It's beautiful."

Naya knew that, in her head. She knew that her parents were proud of their heritage, and any enthusiasm she had for her country and its people came from them. That didn't stop kids named Janet and Stacy from telling her that her name was so *weird*. "You should learn to use other words. Since you write spin for a living, and all."

"Ouch. I also like to tell the truth, you know."

"Then what are you doing working in politics?"

"Technically I'm not, anymore." Ben's coffee was brewed, hot, possibly with milk, and he knocked his knuckles on the large white mug. "I'm in consulting."

"Freelancing."

"Yeah, just like you."

Not *just like her*, because he looked like he was fine, and she was not. Or did she look like that, so hopeful and refreshed, in the first six months of deciding to go on her own? Should she tell him that it won't always be advocacy fun and games, or would that be inevitable so why bother? She was happy for him, if he found purpose.

Was there enough of that to go around?

"I'll get a coffee too." Naya had decided. It was going to rile her up, but maybe she needed that. She was dreading the next stop. Maybe coffee would feel like purpose.

16

"Are you okay?"

"Can I...I need a sec."

Ben would have offered her water or a stiffer drink, but Naya was fine with just placing a hand against the wall and leaning on it. The wall was a textured concrete, there to close off the parking lot from the rest of the block, and not the cleanest of things to lean on.

He had an idea what the next location was, as soon as she said the address. He knew which route to take from Six 32 Central, which roads to skip, where to park. In the car they talked about three things only (eco-bags and how many they had, triclosan avoidance, and how her eyesight was still 20/20), which surprised him because the drive had to have been at least an hour, or longer. He said stuff, and she said stuff, and the car rolled along, and then he was parking. If he could have her around every time he needed to drive anywhere in the city, that would be awesome, universe.

Did he just—yeah, he did think that.

They did not talk about why she was going back to the office she quit in what she said was high drama. He was bringing it up for the first time, there at the parking lot, right before they crossed the street toward *that* building.

"Naya," he said, hopefully sounding as tentative as he felt, "mind if I asked a question?"

"What are we doing here?" She knew, at least. She sighed. "I don't really know."

"What do you mean, you don't know?"

"I mean, I'm here because I need to get something done, and I'm seriously rethinking what it is."

Errand Day flashed back to him, and it wasn't so hard to figure out. The medical exam, the NBI Clearance, and this as the last stop on what would have been a very efficient day, all things considered. "Are you going back in there for a job?"

"God." Like she had sucked on a lemon. "I was trying not to say it aloud for so long, and yes, it sounds very strange. It's like my system wants to reject it."

"But you hated it here."

"I did. I think I still do."

"How are you going to...?"

She blinked at him, with slight annoyance. "I know you understand why, Ben."

There were *other* things she could do, but Ben knew for a fact that most of them, if far enough from the bridges she wanted to burn, would pay her much less. He knew the two-sided conversations happening entirely within one head, when it came to that. He had those thoughts, confronted that same Practical Ben. "Are things different, at least?"

"Same guy's in charge. But my friend got promoted, and I might be working with her instead." Naya's exhale was heavy though. "She said she'll shield me from the bad stuff, as much as she can."

"Naya."

"And it's another consultant job. Not exactly an employer-employee relationship. I can leave, again, if I think I'm being made to cross a line."

"You don't look too happy about this."

"I can't be. I'm settling, is what it is. I've been beaten by the real world, and I'm crawling back to this place. It's what happens."

Was that what happened to him? "I guess it does. But... but you don't need to feel defeated doing it."

"Haha. What does defeat without feeling defeated look like?"

You, Ben wanted to say. Too forward? Too clingy? Too revealing, if he admitted that he actively thought What Would Naya Do as he started this return to All Right? Instead, he pulled his blazer open a little bit, revealing the design on his shirt, right where the left breast pocket would be.

"Oh my God." Naya stepped closer, touched it with her fingers. "What does it say...?"

"*Make Good Days.*" Ben said, taking in the scent of her hair, because she made it close enough to happen. *Make Good Days*, the design said, in beautiful calligraphy, surrounded by blue and green flowers.

"Is it by the same artist?"

"Her contact info was on the card."

"You thought of a better statement. I'm so proud of you."

He thought of her, really, and it was his inside joke to himself and the universe. "But when I had the shirt made I printed it smaller, more discreet, you know."

"Of course. Tasteful. Ben, I...I'm flattered? Should I be?"

"Yes, you should. You know you helped me that day. How can I help you today?"

Naya's face scrunched up, a caricature of discomfort. "I

couldn't tell anybody this, do you know that? I couldn't tell my parents. Melly doesn't know either. Everyone thinks I'm doing okay. 'Aren't you doing what you love?'"

"You were. You still do tours?"

"I do. I also had to wake up and realize that I needed to do it more, like every day, to make sure I could afford to go to the hospital if I get sick. I didn't want to hate what I've been doing. I didn't want to blame it for not being able to take care of me, and buy me things, you know? That's an asshole way to treat your love."

She was absently stroking the Make Good Days design, right there on his chest. "Do you still like it though? Doing the tours?"

"I do. And they're doing well—whenever I pop out a new one, I get paid and it's worth the time and effort. It's still the best paying hobby I've ever had." There was a *but* there, and Ben saw it in her eyes. Instead, she said, "What's your family situation like, Ben?"

"It's just me."

"Because—oh. Seriously? Since when?"

"Almost six years."

Her hand pressed against his chest, a gentle push somewhere near his heart. "I'm sorry. I'm so dramatic lately—I shouldn't have brought it up."

"No, you were about to say something. Tell me."

"I should get over this."

"You said you haven't been able to tell anyone. You can tell me. It's not like I'm one to judge; you know exactly what my rock bottom looked like."

She was still wary, still hesitating.

"Your travel guy. Travel fling. What's it called? Remember? You want to be someone else for a moment, be that with me. It's okay."

"My parents don't have a lot of money," Naya began. "I mean we're okay, but they'll be working all the way to retirement, and they won't have a lot when they do. It's the same for most of my relatives too. Steady jobs that they'll be at until they're old. You know?"

As one of two lawyers in the extended Cacho family, he knew. As the only one who was a writer and worked in government, he also understood the outlier life. "They don't like that you've quit to do tours?"

"Oh, the opposite. They love it. Too much. It's like none of them got to do what they really love, and I rage-quit one day and do this, and they're so *supportive*. They use me as an example of money following passion. They see how much I charge for the tours and they think I'm raking it in, when it's expensive to make sure people are paid well. I can't ask them for help finding a new job...they don't want me to give up on this." Her eyes widened and she looked past him, toward the building, like it was a monster creeping up behind them. "Is that what this is? I've given up?"

"On what? Seems like you haven't."

"I'm walking back into that building to give my clean pee results and NBI Clearance so I could...so I could experience the pleasure of working with these assholes again. But it's not a bad gig, not at all, it's just them. *They* made it difficult for me to keep loving what I do. And I'm going back there. For *money*."

"You need to live the way you want to live."

"I had *principles*." Those eyes swung to him. "You—you have principles. You have them coming out of your ears."

"Yes and you met me when I got thrown under the bus for them. Don't be so hard on yourself."

"Oh *God*." Then she backed up right against the wall, and banged the back of her head on it. Just slightly—not strong enough to injure—but her hand reached for the spot the same time he did. They both hung on, held her together.

"You decide what's right for you, Naya," he said, into her forehead. "Or you stick around long enough to be the last one left."

"You mean out-demon all the demons?"

"That's everyone's game plan, I think."

"There's also this," she said, pulling a folded document from her bag. "Signed this to get my last pay. They refused to accept a signed document online and send the money to me. Said I should drop by for an exit interview first."

"Assholes. It's been years!"

"They like making it difficult."

"But you deserve that last pay anyway."

"Oh I'm getting it whether or not I join them again. It's just...if I work for them again it solves a bunch of my worries."

But piled on new ones. Ben totally understood, and shut up, and took note of the hand that was back on his chest, the head and body now leaning against him.

"You're not a mascot," he told her. "You're under no obligation to live a certain way so people can live vicariously through you."

"People *have* done that. I mean I noticed it when people got so nosy about where I traveled and who I met there. Like they need me to live like that so they won't have to. Will you think I'm a failure if I walk in there and beg for my job back?"

"I can't imagine you being a failure at anything."

"Ben."

She was supposed to say something, and he was supposed to say something, but instead when their lips moved next it wasn't words that happened, but touching, and kissing. A kiss that shouldn't have felt this good, because it was out on the street on a humid, hot day. But it was *that* good, and softer than what he imagined their next kiss would be like, harder than what was appropriate for early afternoon and in public. He brought his hand down from her head to her back, pulling her closer, and in shifting her body against his, everything woke up. His memories, his fantasies of her.

Naya pulled away with a soft gasp. "I have to go in there."

"Of course. Do you need me to...?"

"Yeah. I mean, you can wait somewhere, but inside. I think that would be helpful."

"Whatever you need. But don't go in there feeling weak."

She blinked at him.

"Those monsters. At the museum—that wall of monsters. You're going back in there to face monsters. You need to be one yourself. Which monster are you?"

Naya closed her eyes, like she was seeing them again in her head. "There's one with fireballs for eyes. I like her. I know it's a her. That's me."

"Go get them."

17

The guilt, if it could be called that, had always been there. This wasn't something that took up residence in Naya's gut only within the last year and then grew rapidly to take over her thoughts and actions. Naya had *always* wrestled with this, always lived somewhat creatively among people who weren't. Between bouts of being proud of herself, she would wonder if her success was happening at the expense of others.

That kind of thing followed her all the way from her choice of college major to the way she never called See This Manila a job, or a business.

Income-generating hobby.

No one in her life was asking her to stop doing this. Not in those words. It was, however, in Naya's stubborn nature to keep the "hobby" at arm's length and not completely run with it. When someone like Melly told her to settle down, she never meant to shelve the travel advocacy entirely— often it was supposed to encourage her to commit.

So what was pulling the strings right now, as she sat waiting in the conference room of where she used to work?

Guilt, that she didn't want to eventually have to ask for money from her parents? Resignation, over seeing that she'd come to the point of swallowing pride and crawling back to this circle of hell? How indulgent to even consider this a hardship, when at her age her mother was making sure baby Naya was clothed and fed.

Just smile and sign the contract already. How bad could it be?

"Naya, hey."

She hadn't been sitting for five minutes when the conference room door opened and her friend Alice—thank God—walked in alone. The way Naya's heart thumped with dread over the possibility that it could have been someone else? Not good.

But Alice was good people. She was good at her job, and didn't want to leave it, even when things weren't good. She was a rock and kept Naya together all those times when Naya thought she would quit and then didn't. Alice had the amazing ability to not take home the shit she encountered at work. Not unrelated but she was still around, and now second in command of the whole operation.

That was the main reason why Naya thought it might be okay to come back.

"Alice." Naya gave her a half-hug and a beso. "Hi."

"You're finally here."

"I needed to get the documents together."

"You could have gotten all of it in a day, if you scheduled it."

Truth. "Oh but you know me, my schedule's so all over the place."

Alice was a few years older, probably an entire generation wiser though. "Naya."

"What?"

"You'd tell me if you didn't want this, right?"

"I'm at fifty-fifty, I told you."

"Yes but you're here, which means you've decided which fifty."

"Not necessarily."

Alice took a seat and rolled it closer to Naya's spot, toward the corner of the rectangular table. God, these chairs and their wheels. Naya and Alice used to occupy tables in one room, with a narrow aisle between them. When Naya needed to talk, she'd glide over to Alice's side of the room, and vice versa. It was a tiny thrill to experience it again...to hear the wheels on the floor, to anticipate the words said in confidence.

Tiny thrills got her through the years she spent in this place. Discovering that a job would feel life-draining was to be expected, and after that, she clung to little things that made it even a little fun. Alice. Gossip. That rush of accomplishment after the thing one created turned out exactly as envisioned. Good coffee, most of the time, and office-provided cold water that was inexplicably better than water she had at home.

But mostly gossip.

"Word is they're looking for someone to replace him," Alice hissed.

"*Him?*"

"One and the same."

Naya and Alice's direct project leader—he was called JR in the office—was the reason Naya quit, and the person she had rage-quitted to. Another "little thing" that kept her going, then? The constant murmurs that he would be replaced. That he might be moving on. That they were looking for someone to take over the project instead. But then months would pass and he would still be there. He was always the least-informed in every meeting, but still made the final decisions, still got to throw tantrums and not lose his place.

Many times it was explained to Naya that this wasn't rare, and it happened everywhere. Sad as fuck.

"They've said that a million times," she told her friend. "You still believe it?"

"I've never been deputy before. Never got to see if there were real contenders among the applicants. Or if there even was a job posting out there. And now I've seen them."

"It's real?"

Alice nodded, excited and tense. "It's real. The applications coming in look legit, and a few are frankly from more qualified people. I don't know how real it's going to get when they're negotiating, because I don't think we can afford some of them, but still. It could happen soon, Naya."

"Excuse me if I'm not exactly jumping for joy? Because what the hell is taking so long? Surely something should have eased him out of being the boss long before now. He's the worst guy to lead this thing worth millions and he's still around. Maybe you missed something somewhere? He's not going to let go of this scam. Easiest money he ever made by pretending he knows anything about what this is about. I don't think he's ever going to leave."

"Naya," Alice said, "you have the docs for your employment clearance?"

"I do." There was an NBI clearance laid flat inside a brown envelope, in front of her. She'd be able to send them certification that she was drug-free and medically fit to work. She even had a letter of recommendation from a former media production professor, because they did a project together and was probably Naya's most recent work credential who wasn't Melly and a guest on a tour. This wasn't going to be difficult.

"All you need to do is submit them and sign the contract. Maybe he's here another few months, maybe not. If you want to come back I can make it easier, and maybe it won't be as bad as before."

Naya's side of fifty-fifty, on most days, was to come back. Swallow the pride, smile better, take on another boss tantrum or questionable work order with grace. She was older by a few years; maybe it would be easier.

What kind of day was it, today?

Make good days. The thought popped up, surprising her.

18

C arter Pacific Hotel, 6:15 p.m.

FRESH ORANGE JUICE, that was what she said she wanted. And baked mussels. They seemed to do the trick, because Naya wasn't just laughing, and happy—she was in charge again. Ben had been waiting at the reception area the whole time she was at her meeting. About half an hour later, she emerged, said they should go.

He asked her how it went, but she said she didn't want to talk about it. And she said she wanted orange juice and baked tahong.

"I think what we can conclude here," she was saying, "is that you're kind of bad at scheming, and I have to do this."

"I came up with the plan! Well, some of it."

"I had to fix most of it, even in this planning stage. This isn't a heist movie, Ben."

Wasn't it? It looked like one to him. The lounge of the

Carter Pacific was where the adults at this hotel went for drinks, but it was designed like they were in a scene from a sci-fi dystopian film. A *heist* sci-fi dystopian film, and this was when the well-dressed minions plotted to steal from their overlords. Gray, shiny columns all around them curved, merged into reflective walls, creating pockets of space that seemed private enough. Ben could hear female voices; live performers singing on the other side of the closest wall, but the sound was muffled somehow, not intrusive. He could talk to Naya and hear her, and feel assured that the other tables wouldn't hear them. He could barely see them too.

"It's like stealing," he said dryly. "I think of it as stealing my job back."

"Based on how you tell it, you weren't supposed to lose that job."

"You believe me, don't you?"

She smirked. "That's the question, isn't it? I've only spent two days with you. Barely."

"Touché." The baked mussels were excellent, by the way, an explosion of mussel and garlic and cheese in his mouth. She liked it; he liked it. How many dishes would they have to eat together, would he have to watch her taste, for them to feel okay with this? What was the acceptable number of days to know someone, before trusting them with your career? Maybe not two. Ben worked very efficiently, he liked to think. No days wasted. "But still, you probably have a better handle on what happened to my job than even I do."

"You're very trusting, Ben."

"I'm not, Naya."

"Did you look me up before you got back in touch? Checked me out, if I lied to you about anything?"

"I looked you up, sure, but not for those reasons. I just missed you."

Naya lifted the fancy, slim glass to her lips and said nothing.

He continued, "And nothing you said to me contradicted what I saw, when I looked you up. That sunset series, that was awesome."

"Thank you."

"That video you did, right after the summit, when you went to the places behind the motorcade barriers they put up—it was excellent."

"Oh, that." She exhaled and it was heavy. "The reason why they held my last pay. They wanted me to take that down. It's weird—I mean that video still took two weeks from end to end to do, you know? It wasn't an impulsive thing. It takes work to wake up and get up and do that thing for days and not think you're making a mistake that'll anger your ex-boss and have him ransom your salary."

"I didn't know that. I never saw the video before, but it wasn't inconsistent. No lies." On the contrary, seeing Naya's principles in action, seeing her slightly younger self demonstrating passion, made him feel things during his own rock bottom. Like hope. "Did anything about how my resignation was covered make you change your mind about me?"

She was chewing, and she made him wait for her answer. She chewed slowly, thoughtfully, tapped her fingertips on her lips before licking them and finally speaking. "No."

"Great. That's all?"

"I looked you up too. I was looking you up while we're in the van, on the day you walked into it. You were...all right. I mean, based on what I saw."

"I'm not lying about anything."

"What's your phrase...*not inconsistent.* And give me some credit; I don't regret what we did."

"Thank God." *Thank God.*

"And I'm flattered you'd come to me for help."

"You are on top of my list of trustworthy and capable people."

"I'm kind of concerned about that, because you should know better people."

He shrugged. "I do know people. I also know I can't trust them."

"Ben. Is this job really worth stealing back then?"

"I told you it is." He told her, in the car on the way to the hotel, and then in the hotel as they waited for their order, and during another famous Manila Bay sunset, that this was his epiphany, and what he decided after he got out of his funk. He believed in what he was doing, in what he could do, and he was not going to do it for anyone else. David Alano did not deserve to have Elmo Laranas running his comms. For the past two months, Ben began working for his mentor Tana Cortes, and the first step to making sure Elmo was replaced was getting David into a meeting with Tana. Something Ben couldn't do himself—both he and Tana were pretty much blacklisted from David's office. "Elmo has been the rot on that ship for years, and he keeps insisting he's needed. He's not."

"Tana can't just call David?"

"She won't."

"They can't just set up a regular meeting? She has a legit consulting company."

"They can't be seen together. Not yet, not while Elmo's in the picture."

"But we have to make sure they meet in person."

"She'll be able to convince him of things, in person."

"God, you people are messed up." Then things clicked for Naya, and her eyes widened with glee. "They fuck, don't they? Silver Fox Senator and your Boss Woman. Oh my God."

Ben was drinking apple juice, also in a fancy slim glass, and nearly choked on his last gulp. Because he had assumed that, yes, though not in those words. Inappropriate to think of his ex-boss, and his mentor and new boss, but... "They're involved. I don't know. Maybe."

"Wow. They totally are. What kind of wild campaign were you guys running?"

"A successful one, thank God," Ben admitted. "We were polling in the middle, but it was enough. It did get tense a lot, because of Tana and Elmo. Tana and David met in school overseas, a long time ago. She was working for a non-profit and he brought her in for comms. It was his first national campaign, and she's good. She really is."

"And Elmo?"

"Elmo...had money. Or knew people with money. He knows how they speak, what they respond to. You can imagine they had arguments."

"That, and Tana and the Candidate were involved."

"No one knew that for sure, okay? I mean, they were never demonstrative. She was probably harder on him than anyone else. And they were working together. And Tana's got a kid, with another guy. Can't two people be platonic friends for over a decade?"

"Is she still with the baby daddy?"

"I don't think so."

Naya's eye roll was a wide and visible arc even in the dim lounge light. "Fine, maybe they're not. But if they are, it's too bad they have to hide it. Can't two people who have complicated lives fuck sometimes in secret and maybe it's no one else's business?"

Now that she mentioned it, that segment of Ben's life flashed before his eyes, and of course the possibility was likely. He knew some of the staff gossiped about them, and he tried to stay out of it. How things had changed—now he was in the middle of it, orchestrating a reunion of sorts between the two.

So he could get his job back.

"I understand why Elmo would stay and Tana would go." Naya's words cut into his flashback sequence. "Because guys like that thrive on proximity to power. No matter how gross their methods. And you think if Tana were to replace him, things would be better?"

"You can look her up. Her track record is stellar, and she's taught me everything I know."

And then she was doing it; typed a search, tapped on photos, read some pages. They had some time before David was expected at the hotel, and...this was probably their first date. Technically.

"She's gorgeous." Naya held her phone to him discreetly, showing him a recent photo of Tana. "I ship."

"They're my bosses. But...but whatever makes them happy, I guess." But if they did do *that*—if David and Tana were in that kind of relationship for that long—how did they stand being apart? The other relationships, the proximity of working together forcing emotional distance, the stress of it all? "Do you think...? I don't know."

"Do I think what?"

"You'll think it's corny."

"You don't know what I'll think." She straightened up in her seat, all the better to survey the round table between them, holding the plate of tahong shells and a glass of juice and water each. "Spit it out, Ben."

"Do you think people can just do that? Be classic drama love-of-their-lives and then decide to stay apart?"

She frowned, making a tiny crease on her forehead. "Yes, two people can just do that. They can do whatever they want. Sounds like their lives aren't so fun, and maybe it's not the healthiest thing to stay together. I don't know, maybe it makes sense to fuck once in a while but keep it at that."

"But what if they're good together?"

Naya shrugged. "They're like, forty by now, right? They've been at this longer than us, maybe they know something we don't."

All of these were acceptable, and correct. The last thing Ben would recommend as someone on a senator's comms staff was to draw attention to the senator's sex life. The same way Ben would never have trashed Jacqueline Buena for her decision to have a kid. All of these were fine.

But when you find someone who fires up all sides of yourself, what do you do? *Fuck once in a while and keep it at that* seemed disrespectful.

"See?" He said instead. "You think it's corny."

"I think you need practice being sneaky. I can't even believe I'm telling a lawyer and a senator's speechwriter this, but the best thing for you is for me to do the thing tonight. You're too earnest."

"You mean I like telling the truth."

"That is so precious. How come you only got thrown under the bus this year? You should stay here and let me do the rest."

19

L iving in one place for so long made one feel all its walls and corners, sure, and whenever someone complained to her that they were finding their city too "small," Naya was always quick with a recommendation for where to go to breathe. Usually it meant a bus or plane ride, or a long drive. Sometimes, for emergencies, other places would do. It wasn't about how far away, but which world to enter.

The Carter Pacific, and many hotels in Manila like it, catered to business travelers and families with money to burn. Not her usual world, though some days she had to step into it, for work. If Ben couldn't help but be exactly who he was in every single world of his home city, Naya had no problem tweaking her settings to feel more at home in this one.

She spotted the senator as soon as he came into the lounge. They seated him and the other guy by the huge bay windows. They were served glasses of water; the other guy had a beer. The way the shiny wall curved around them, Naya could barely see the other guy, but at least from her new spot at the bar, she could tell that David was still at the table. Then the other guy stood up, his phone to his ear, and the senator was alone.

Good job, Ben's friend. Naya needed to be quick about this, but also not scary. Her approach to the senator's table was measured, and her smile bright. "Good evening, Senator Alano. Hope you don't mind my saying hello. My name is Naya, and I'm a friend of Ben Cacho."

Close like this, and with sexy lounge lighting, Naya had to admire the man she had been appropriately calling Silver Fox all day. He stood up, and offered a hand for her to shake. "Ben, yes, it's been a while. How is he?"

"Good, good," Naya said. "He has a message for you."

She handed him a piece of paper, folded once. The senator read it and she could tell he knew what it meant— he gave a small nod and slipped it into his pants pocket.

"That's all," Naya said. "Thank you, and I should go."

"Wait. Naya. How is he, really?"

"He's okay."

"How long have you known him?"

Got me there. "Not long. But he's okay."

"I tried to get in touch with him during—" His voice trailed off, and then he pushed both hands into his pockets. "But this is good, it should be good. If they're working together, then he's good. She'll take care of him."

"I hope so. I hope..." Oh God. It wasn't her place at all, and it wasn't even her character. She had approached him as Naya if she were in this world, just another business traveler, a subdued version of herself. But but but: "I hope you find the backbone to take care of him too."

"What did you say?"

"I *said* he's good at his job and he has fucking integrity, and that's the kind of person you keep on your side, instead of rewarding the ones who make deals with all the little and big devils. Because that says something about *you*, sir, when you make it hard for people like him to stay. And people like him are the only ones who keep things going, who make sure people don't get screwed more, who make sure the house doesn't completely burn just yet. It's *hard* to keep people around who want to do that. And when the last of them give up, what becomes of us?"

Oh God. She said that. She said that?

To his credit, he took this better than her ex-boss did. David Alano's eyes were kind; his face didn't contort into a defensive mask. "Is that what you think is happening?"

"It's—it's not inconsistent."

"Do you think it's that simple? Everyone has good intentions."

"No, not everyone." Naya felt the seething, the blood rushing to her face. What a horrible thing, to be reunited with your own monster self. "Sir, I'm not a child. And fuck that—we teach kids to be kind, and giving, and decent. We should expect adults to have learned how to do that at *some* point along the way. I've been in similar spaces. I know what it feels like. Stop killing compassion in people. Hell, stop killing *passion* in people. You can see what it's doing to everything. Unless you don't, because it's completely gone in you now."

Dear Lord. Rage-quit Naya. Where was the wise one, the cynic? Where was Naya from ten freaking minutes ago?!

"That's all," she said, struggling to find her composure. "Thank you for your time."

"Naya," David said. "I think we've worked together before."

"I don't think so—"

Recognition dawned on his face. "The PH Lens project.

We didn't meet in person but I was on its steering committee, and I watched everything. You were very good in that."

Shit—not only did she transform into exact incarnation
of who she was years ago, he recognized her too.
"Thank you."

"Thank you as well."

And then she ran out of there.

~

WHAT DID SHE JUST DO?

On the day she quit her job, Naya felt no regret. She
liked to call it a "rage-quit" and surely it seemed like it to
anyone who was there. On most days she was bubbly, quiet,
chill. She had enthusiasm even when she wasn't filming
herself, and during disagreements, she sometimes argued
but never lost her cool.

Inside was a different story. Inside, Naya argued with
herself dozens of times, before speaking up. Debated
constantly with herself if this was a battle she really wanted
to fight, then learned to start shutting up, without actually
wanting to. Months upon months of that led to what
she did.

Not unlike the lecture she just gave to a senator.

Yikes, she just did that.

When she got back to Ben, still panting from running,
he asked her how it went. And the truth was, it was peachy.
All good. She gave him the note, he read it, and they weren't
discovered. What happened next was all up to the good
senator; Ben and Naya did their part.

Still, she felt like getting out of there as soon as possible.
"It's done, let's go." She all but pulled him off the seat,

leaving him to scramble to leave cash on the table, enough to cover their bill.

"What do you mean, it's done?" He was letting her drag him out, sure, but he kept asking. "He got the note?"

"Yes."

"He read it? He understood it?"

"Yes. I think so? Yes. Let's *get out of here.*"

"What happened? Did Elmo see you?"

"He didn't."

The glass doors slid open and they stepped out onto the driveway, then the street. It had been hot all day; now in the middle of the evening, the sky was starless and it smelled like rain soon. *Take shelter.* Briefly she used it as her excuse to walk fast, to keep going, as if they were seconds away from downpour. She was at least two steps ahead of him going up the block, in the direction of where he parked the car. If she had her way she'd fly—she truly felt like she had exposed herself to something in there, and she couldn't get away fast enough.

"Naya. Hey."

"In the car."

"Hey."

"Let's talk *in the car.*"

"Did he say anything to you?"

What part of *let's talk in the car...?* Naya tried to give him her best Everything's Fine face. "He didn't say anything. I mean, he said things, but not bad things."

He was giving her his best Concerned Face. Then a Concerned Hand had gently settled on her wrist. When she welcomed his touch and leaned toward him, the Concerned Arm brought her closer. "Was it wrong to ask you to help today? I don't know what happened there. If you were threatened or hurt—"

"I'm not hurt. He didn't threaten me. I..."

I need a hug. They were halfway there anyway, with the arms, so she hugged him. What she felt right away was a disorienting comfort. Naya *gave* hugs, she realized, *gave* comfort through the hug. She hadn't really felt *this* in a long time. When her hand curved around his nape, when she pressed her lips against his, *she* got something out of it. *She* felt better, in bursts. She hoped the feeling was mutual, that she wasn't inadvertently taking something from him, but Ben kissed her back like he had all warmed up and was ready to go.

"Your place," she decided. He was okay with that. It wasn't the closest location but she didn't have any hotel strings to pull that night and not her place, not where she was living with her cousin, because too many questions.

So they went back to where they started that morning, the Six 32 Central neighborhood, and to one of the buildings on the fringes of the business district, coincidentally one that she was familiar with because she briefly considered living there. She would have, too, if she had a better job or didn't quit the one she had. Who'd have thought years later she'd get to test it out? Life was like that sometimes.

So far, so good, by the way. Seemed secure enough. An elevator that required a card to exit on specific floors. Well-lit hallway, clean and shiny floors. If she lived there maybe she would have had reason to shut up, to stay, because rent was a huge part of her monthly expenses and sometimes the decision was to pay more for a better escape. Naya was thinking about this in the seconds it took to walk down the hall, but everything left her head as soon as they made it into his apartment.

Ben's place. Was it new? How long had he been living here? Many things about the space seemed new, primarily that it wasn't a mess. Not at all, and when he dropped his blazer over the dark wood dining table it seemed like clutter, like it didn't belong there.

For too many days than she cared to admit, she thought about this. About him, about the next time. It wasn't healthy to expect it. She'd let herself indulge this time, please.

He kissed her cheek first. Open-mouthed, gentle, like he was taking a tentative bite. It was...unexpected? And sweet. Naya responded with the same, an open-mouthed kiss on his collarbone, sweeping toward his throat.

Too many clothes.

"Bedroom?" Ben's voice was a sexy whisper, or maybe it was because they were still too close to the front door. She nodded and didn't wait to be led; was two steps ahead of him toward it too.

His bed wasn't made. That was fine, no one was perfect after all. She didn't mind so much that she was seeing what his bedroom really looked like, on a normal day. Like he had just gotten up, gone to work, no time to fold the sheets and plump the pillows.

Travel flings for Naya weren't *just* one-night stands. There were second nights, and mornings, and sometimes more. She couldn't recall a second night happening months later, with all the daydreams and fantasies starring this guy in between. Truth—when he pulled his shirt off and she touched the bare skin of his chest with her open palm, she felt ready to combust.

Not come, though. Not just yet. She hadn't planned a second time with Ben but now that it was here, she was going to make it count. The dynamic was different the first time; not as playful as she would have wanted. She had a feeling this time he'd allow a bit more...curiosity.

So far, he'd let her do what she wanted. She had

stripped him down to his boxers. He waited, his breath quick, as she shed her top and pants, only leaving on her pale pink bra and black panties. He let her position him, on his back on the bed, only groaning in near pain when she straddled him between her legs, sitting right on his thighs.

This would be a new view for him. They hadn't gotten to do this with him under her. She was liking how this felt already, liking the warmth from where their legs touched. She liked his body, wondered what he did to keep in shape. They had a gym in the building, she knew. Did he use it? How often? Not *too* often maybe. She pressed a fingertip against his abs and hoped he saw her appreciation. No six-pack just yet but she liked how it felt, remember how it looked when he was all tensed up, thrusting into her. It was a good body, congratulations, she especially liked how it moved.

He was wearing his glasses, still. Ben tried to discard them but she stopped him. She liked them on him, not going to apologize.

"If you remove your glasses...?"

"I can see," he replied. "I just won't be...able to read. Certain text sizes. From certain distances."

"Hmm." She liked the idea that he'd be able to see everything, clearly. "Keep them on."

"Okay."

Naya touched his abs again, using the same fingers, then trailed down lower, over the waistband of his boxers, up the bulge that strained against the fabric. She felt it move, under her touch. Hello. "May I see it?"

"Yes." He had grabbed the blanket; she liked the clenched fists and the flexed forearms. She liked the restraint, that she didn't have to ask for. Sometimes it happened like this—she'd take control and a lover would let her. Always fun. "What do you need me to do?"

"Just watch." Naya's hand slipped into the flap in his boxers, fingers wrapping around him. So...she liked this too? Another thing not to apologize for. She hadn't been able to *touch* as much, that first time. But now he was in her hand, feeling hard and smooth and... "Do you get tested? Like, regularly?"

"Y-yes. I did. I'm okay. And—and no one else since you."

That was unexpected information. She didn't know how to feel about that, so she just went ahead with what she was going to ask anyway. "May I use my mouth?"

"Fuck."

He was cute when he was like this. Naya closed her fingers around him and stroked down, to the root of him, then up, slow. "That's not an answer."

"Fuck. *Yes.*"

He was cute when he remembered words. Naya slid her body down his legs, got comfortable, then wrapped her lips around the tip of his cock. There, first, with her tongue, then more of him. Once, she glanced up at him and he was looking right at her, lusty and helpless, and another time he had closed his eyes, thrown his glasses away somewhere.

He's hot, was what she was thinking, almost counterintuitive given their position, but the heat Naya felt, the near-combustion, it was still there. It hadn't taken her over; she was using it. She used it with her hands, her tongue, how she closed her lips around him. The sounds he made got her hotter, had her touching herself, had her completely ready and wet and not caring whether it was too soon to come.

The next words he formed were a warning that he was about to do just that, and she decided not in her mouth, not today. *So hot*, she thought, as she watched him come, sort of gasp and groan in helpless abandon, and she brought herself there too.

"You okay?" She giggled. He gave a slight, exhausted nod in response. So cute, the way he looked a little destroyed.

20

Naya didn't leave right after, so Ben allowed himself to relax. He used the bathroom to clean up after she did, and when he was done, he found her on his bed, legs draped over a pillow. Pink bra, black panties—interesting color combination. He felt like his bedroom suddenly transformed into a magazine centerfold, or a photo shoot location, some glamorous place in another dimension.

"It's still early." It was exactly what he was thinking, that he maybe shouldn't have said aloud.

"I know."

There was a hint of a giggle there, which was a small comfort, made stronger by how her arms went around him when he joined her on the bed. Her lips grazed his brow, and he needed to kiss her, hadn't kissed her enough.

"Ben," she said. "Your bed is really nice."

"Glad you noticed." He picked it himself. The condo wasn't furnished when he got it, and beds mattered to him. Because of sleeping really, although now he congratulated himself on making good decisions.

"I sleep on a futon in a living room. I'm sure it's bad for my spine. Melly has the bedroom and the actual bed."

"Lie down flat then. And stretch."

That got him a brief side-eye from her, like she was checking if he was joking, and then she shrugged it off and did it anyway. Turned to face the ceiling, raised her arms over her head, and stretched. A small sigh escaped her mouth as her body made a straight line, pointed toes to stretched fingers.

"You're on your feet all day," he said. "Must be tough on your body."

"More now than it used to be. And my voice too."

"You should take care of yourself."

"I know. Do you want to do something about it?"

Something inside him stirred. Arousal, that was what it was. He had work the next day but—"Whatever you want."

"Are you sure? Maybe you aren't ready."

"Try me." *What are you saying? You just blew a load and you aren't twenty-four anymore.* And yet the need for her grew, so maybe his confidence wasn't going to fail him.

"I was wondering if you could do slow."

"Slow?"

"Lazy Sunday afternoon kind of sex."

"Maybe you should explain what Sunday afternoons are like for you."

"When you don't want to move from your bed," she said, her eyelids heavy. "When you tell yourself it's okay, because it's hot outside, and you're feeling a gentle breeze from somewhere, and you have work tomorrow so you just want the afternoon to last forever."

Oh, that was what Sunday was for a lot of people? He hadn't had that in years. "I thought you worked in tourism."

"I *freelance*. I reclaimed my Sundays."

"Not Thursday rush hour sex then."

Her laugh rolled over his skin, he could swear it did. "Slow but unsatisfying, makes you angry?"

"No one should put you through that. Never, ever."

"You say really nice things to me."

"I don't lie."

He didn't know if she was going to say something, or sigh—his mouth captured hers, and stayed there. She wanted slow and he could do that. He let the kiss last as long as his held breath. Spent a leisurely stretch of time just exploring her mouth with his tongue. They'd never really done slow, but this was perfect, he could do this. He felt like he was slowly melting, being consumed by her, when in fact it was his body atop hers, his mouth doing the tasting. And he felt himself getting ready for her again, but if she wanted slow then that was what she would get. More of everything for him. More time. More to touch.

Naya had a tan line on her arm, right where the short sleeve of a shirt would end. It didn't make a difference, when it came to how the skin tasted or felt. What it did was remind him of what she was wearing on the day they met. Their first day. Their only other day.

"Slow enough for you?" He remembered to check.

"Perfect," she murmured.

He explored her elbows, her wrists, the slight curve under her breasts, the spheres her nipples became. Fingers first, then tongue, for everything. He wasn't slow, necessarily. He thought of it as lingering, staying, discovering what he hadn't before. She was wet now, and ready, but he wanted to linger there too. Gently, he stroked her where she was wet. "Here?"

"Yes."

Fingers, then tongue there too. He heard whimpers but

they were like commands, telling him where to go, what to do. She came around his fingers; graceful in his eyes even as she panted and all but cried out.

"You okay?" He pressed a kiss against her thigh. "You want more?"

"Yes more."

"You want it slow?"

"Still slow, yes. You think you can handle it?"

He laughed at the challenge but really, this was a test and he couldn't believe he was doing well at it. Not when he knew as soon as she asked for a quick fuck he'd switch gears and it would be so fucking quick. But he did as he was told, as was expected. He wore the latex and slowly, slowly pushed inside her. Pushed in deep, and held.

"So *good*." She said that.

"Yeah?" It felt decadent, lazy. He did want to stay there for hours, for the whole day, never leave. He didn't want to think about work the next day, the things he was supposed to do. He pulled out slowly, almost completely, and then slid back in again, deep. "Fuck."

"*Yes*. Like that."

Like that, until each stroke was delicious but also painful, until her moans became more and more urgent.

"Tell me," he grunted into her ear. "Tell me if you want it harder."

"I will."

"Tell me if you want to fuck now."

"I will."

Another slow stroke, and he willed himself not to come, not until she got what she wanted, not yet—

Naya laughed and it was the best sound. In the top three of all sounds in the world. "Now. Now. Okay, harder, now."

Then it was hard, and very, very fast.

~

BEN WOKE up because his elbow was shaking. No, because it was being tapped, very lightly. Naya was sitting, fully dressed, on a chair beside his bed. He did not have a chair there; she had brought in the one from the dining area. This confused him for a second.

"Good morning," he said.

"Hi. I didn't want to leave without saying goodbye."

That...is not ominous at all. "How about we get something to eat? I don't have to be at work until—" But he wasn't sure what time it was, and his phone wasn't where it usually was.

"Ben." Naya was sitting cross-legged, and he wondered how long she'd been awake before he got his tap. "I didn't ask for my job back, yesterday."

"Oh. Oh. But you didn't want to work there again anyway?"

"I didn't. I didn't know what else to do, either. You kind of found me again right when I was swallowing my pride for once. I might have signed a contract and gotten an epic I Told You So if you hadn't suddenly appeared."

He felt sore and sleepy but this needed his attention and he pushed himself to sitting. "Is that a bad thing? I can't tell if you think it's a bad thing."

"I don't know. It's just...I thought I was doing something yesterday that would help me out, and then all I did was take my last pay and leave. I still don't have a job. I'm—I'm not sure what I'm supposed to do. And I'm sorry."

"Sorry for what?" No, no, she should not be apologizing. Not for last night, not for anything.

"Yesterday I was supposed to do boring errand stuff. Get documents. Get my job back. I ended up telling them I didn't want my stinking job back. I yelled at a senator. And I had sex with you when...when..."

She yelled at David? What? How? But Ben needed that last part even more. "When what? What about sex with me?"

"When I was having a bad day."

"There's nothing wrong with that." As far as he was concerned, nothing wrong with that at all. He'd been on board with everything she wanted to do, whatever she needed it for. "Good days, bad days, just tell me what you need."

"You're not a travel fling. Do you get it? You're not. You're a great guy who's smart and principled and great in bed and you live like half an hour away from me. I shouldn't use you to fill voids in my life."

"You're making it sound bad. You helped me when I had a really bad day."

"I know, I know, and I had an excuse for it. But I can't use the travel fuck excuse now."

"Why does it sound like you're dumping me?"

"It's not spin. I'm frankly taken aback by you, you're like a unicorn in government. And not in a bad way—I think you do what you can, and you're not above mistakes, but you seem to be willing to fix things."

"So what's so wrong with that? With this?"

She raised an eyebrow, calling forth the spirit of the strict teacher he first saw her as. "Excuse me. It took you five months before you contacted me again. And why?"

"Because I didn't want you to see me at rock bottom."

"Yes."

"But what if I want to be around to help you."

"What if, that's not a thing you get to decide?"

That stung, because truth.

She added, "You had your time; it's fair that I have mine.

I'd like the chance to fix things without having someone watch and wait."

"Why are you telling me not to wait?"

Me, like she had said it directly to him, when she'd said *someone* like it could have been anyone. He wasn't overreaching. It was a completely reasonable assumption given the circumstances. It was also totally, completely a whine.

Worse, he had more whine: "Don't you think we have something special here? I wasn't even *looking* for someone. For anyone. I'm so used to dealing with every fucking life emergency alone and then—and then you. And it felt *great,* Naya."

"Maybe it's just nice to get yourself an orgasm on a really bad day, Ben. Don't we know that already?"

"That's not what it is. Well, maybe just some of it. But not all of it. I want to spend the good days and bad days with *you.*"

For a second, Ben wished he had relationship experience. The kind that lasted longer than the two months of dating, hooking up a few times, then calling it quits because he could never really say he would be done by eight or free on Saturday. Because when *they* said to him they'd had enough, he let them walk away. Law school, then work, that was everything to him at those times. And all that work had saved him when he wasn't sure how to deal with his grief. He was productive during loss, or maybe it helped him deal.

"Naya," he said. "If you want to leave because you don't think I can handle it, please reconsider. I don't mind learning how to be better at this. I think—I think we're great together, we just need to spend more time actually being together."

"I agree," she said, her voice soft and apologetic. "But I don't think the time is now."

"Why not now? We're both here."

"It's not up for debate, Ben."

He felt a vibration on the bed. His phone had buzzed, notifying him of a text message. And another. And another. He didn't want to take his eyes off her but it sounded urgent.

"I think it's there. Under the pillow." She pointed with her finger and uncrossed her legs.

"Just a second. Don't leave yet."

A series of messages, from Tana. He grudgingly read them. Okay, this was important news.

"What's up?" Naya asked.

"I...have my job back." Ben almost couldn't believe it. "Our scheme worked."

"What—really?"

"Yeah. Tana's the senator's new chief of staff. I'm back on the comms team. Elmo's been let go. Shit, I suddenly have a job."

"See?" Naya straightened up, her body language all but announcing her exit. "This is going to be another big change. It's not a good time for you either."

"Maybe it's not about perfect timing," he said. "Maybe it's just always going to be levels of shitty, Naya. I still think it'll be great for us if we were in this together."

"You have to give me time to come to that conclusion, you know. Since we're both adults here. I should go."

He didn't want her to go. An outline for a longer speech was forming in his head, an entire argument he felt he could win. About how her passion was contagious, how he was only able to do what he did because he thought of what she would do. What would Naya do. And if being around him spurred any kind of feeling, got her to take any kind of action...wouldn't that be good for her too? He could cite examples. Memories. He'd be able to quote things she'd said, proof that trying it out together was better than staying apart. If she was going through the exact same funk he was in the past few months, maybe he was in a position to help. If she'd let him.

But...it wasn't a debate.

"I'm going," she said.

He nodded reluctantly. He couldn't say yes; it was as if saying the word meant he agreed with her. "What did you tell David?"

"Hmm?"

"You said you yelled at the senator. What did you tell him?"

Naya cringed. "Something about getting a backbone. How he's supposed to keep hope alive in people like you, but he failed you."

This made him feel good, and warm, and impressed. David did not get yelled at often. He wished he had seen it. No doubt it influenced the events that followed, that he was now benefiting from. "I think you helped make this happen, Naya. What just happened—it's a big deal."

"Oh, sure. It's either my little outburst, or the night he just spent with his Secret Lover Boss Woman. This is still sneaky risky business, your world. I'm not sure if an idealistic rant helped anything at all."

"You know what I mean, Naya. You make good days."

She pushed herself off the chair, brought her face close enough that he felt her peppermint-scented sigh. "For other people, I guess. That's my specialty. I'm glad I gave you another good day, Ben. You really are a great person."

One last kiss, lips against cheekbone, and then she left.

Good thing he had a job again, a real one, because he needed to channel that productivity from loss somewhere.

21

"I love you."

"Thanks, Melly."

"Even when you're being stubborn as shit."

What would she do without her cousin? Best friend, practically a sister, sometime business partner and driver, now roommate. Naya wasn't sure what she brought to the table. Yay for being related? Naya was probably given a lot more patience than Melly's other friends. "Gee, thanks."

"I didn't even know that going back to the old job was on the table. You were miserable."

Yes, and Melly would remember that, because Naya complained about it often enough. It was a miracle that the ranting hadn't seeped into her own videos. "Alice kept telling me that things were going to change soon."

"Alice has like the highest tolerance for bullshit I've ever heard of. You were waiting for a management change at that place for years."

"I thought it was me," Naya admitted. "For so long I thought it was me. That I needed an attitude adjustment.

Because other people were there and they could do it, and maybe I could too if I just...stopped caring."

"Naya. You can talk to me about this. I mean if it's work, we can figure it out."

"Excuse me, Little Miss Business Major."

"Double major. And another degree on the way. But it shouldn't be the choice between having absolutely no income or going back to the toxic workplace that rewarded mediocre men. I'm sure we can find better options for you than that dystopia. Will you let me help?"

That was a misrepresentation; Melly had always helped. Every iteration of Naya's career, even this one where she was crashing on her cousin's couch. "I know you've been doing that all this time."

"I'm cool that way."

"I love you."

"Thanks, Naya. Can we shift the topic back to Ben though?" Melly peeled the paper wrapper off her egg sandwich, purchased there at the café, and took her first bite, chewing silently.

"Aren't you late for work or something?" Naya asked. She didn't think she'd catch her cousin at home at all. On a school day, Melly was out of there before eight. They'd run into each other at the lobby as Melly was heading out, and now they were parked at the café across the street for sandwiches and coffee and words. Naya had quickly mentioned where she'd come from, but then she was able to change the subject.

Not for long, apparently.

"I have time," Melly said. "All afternoon classes today. And I never catch you on a morning walk of shame—no wait, that's not what we call it. What do we call it again?"

"Nothing. Late night, that's all."

"Right." Melly giggled. "But this is rare, so I'm here if you want to make your 'late night' my business."

"There will be no other business with him, I said."

"Naya."

"Melly."

"Amansinaya."

"Pamela Grace."

Melly bit into her sandwich again. "Well, you're an adult. I guess you know what you're doing. I mean, he works in politics. Yuck. Of course you won't want to see *that* again."

Naya shrugged, then sipped from her coffee cup.

Melly went on, "And you know they're all the worst. I mean, you worked there. You quit what would have been a dream job because of them. They're all the same. You even helped him heist his way back into his old job. Because people can't write proper resignation and application letters? Can't trust people who work in that system at all, if you ask me."

What could Naya say to that? So she just blinked.

"And," her cousin said, index finger on the table for emphasis, "how old is Ben? Early thirties? That means he only has a few years left."

"A few years left of what?"

"Of looking like a hottie. He'll hit forty then he'll start looking like them. Trapos all look like, it's wild. I think there's a memo and a uniform and also required photo poses."

They *both* thought that. "Melly."

"I'm helping you feel better about your life, Naya. Maybe you're right to walk away. Don't think '*not all trapos*' with this guy. Maybe he is just like them, or he will be."

"I love that you're making sense but it's so early."

Melly smirked at her. "It's late, for you, because you're

super tired from all your *business*. I'm perfectly awake. But okay, I'm trying to understand why *not* him. You just—it's new, and it should be okay to make mistakes sometimes. You literally spent only *two days* together."

I don't want him to become a mistake. Naya's eye twitched, from the thought, and Melly noticed, so now she had to say something. "He seems like a great guy and I don't want him to be someone's mistake. Not mine, first of all."

"Wow. He's that pure? He can't be."

"It doesn't matter. The adult thing to do is to step back."

Step back, remember that she didn't need this, remember that he had his own completely separate thing going on and if they couldn't manage to make their lives intersect and fit years ago, it was not realistic to think they could do that now. She learned this from experience. Adults learned things from when they were younger, duh.

"You really do believe all that independence stuff, don't you?" Melly asked.

Naya remembered that Melly had been in a long-term relationship for most of her twenties. They'd broken up before they turned thirty, and this was Melly's second year of being single and it was probably the longest stretch since she started dating. The mindset was just *different*. "What are you talking about?"

"The cousins, everyone else—they love you, but they think you're kidding yourself about the travel flings. Like, you're never going to 'find a man' that way."

"I never said that's what it was for."

"I know, I know. But you know how families don't believe you? Or they think you're on this sad downward spiral of sex and self-esteem issues? It's not just you, honey, but you too."

Oh, she was aware. She was lucky that it was easy for

her; she had always thought her independence was a feature, not a fallback. "Still, it's none of their business."

"Yes, I think I get that now about you. I used to think you were hooking up while traveling because you were lonely. Or you were lonely, and that's why you traveled and hooked up. But it's not that simple, is it?"

"I'm not lonely."

"I'm beginning to understand it. And you've always told us that, but it's easy to not believe you. You have been queen of doing things for yourself, ever since. I also know that if you want something, you can get it done."

I make good days. "I guess I do."

She did *do that.* Naya was not in her element lately, but maybe it was a funk she'd get over soon? The travel business could become sustainable. She could transition it into something she could do, while she worked on something that would take better care of her. She could think of these things, and not freak out, and not go running back to toxic environments.

If she could do it for others, surely she could do it for herself.

But Melly was not done. "Can I just say something?"

"You will anyway."

"If you need someone, that can be okay too. You can't expect to solve your own shit all the time."

Not exactly what she wanted to hear after her personal pep talk. "It shouldn't be anyone's responsibility to do that but mine."

"Yeah yeah—but sometimes we do that for each other? You know you can stay on my futon as long as you like."

"I know that."

"You know we can put our heads together and solve that job problem if you really want my help."

Naya's breath came out, coffee-scented, sounding like a hiss. "Sure."

"And...and if there's an interesting guy who wants to spend time with you, and you like him too...maybe you should do that. Maybe. Just a suggestion."

"It's not a good time to do that right now."

"Yeah...but you know how it is with other independent people, right? Independent people with interesting lives just like you? They have their own schedules too. You might miss a moment, and if you don't speak up, you'll lose them because they'll be off on their own way."

Which is the exact point of the travel fling. And letting go of your travel fling. And not letting yourself think it's going to work, when it's back to the real world, your world, which is worrying about bills and health care and lining up at dull places.

Melly felt that she scored a major point and dabbed a tissue on her lips, looking smug. "Compromising's so annoying."

"Shut up."

"Anyway, you'll always have me."

22

I n the daytime, the lounge at the Carter Pacific looked less sci-fi dystopia, and more...hotel lounge. Even though the walls remained, it seemed sunnier, more open, not as many corners to hide in.

Not going to lie, Ben felt relief when he showed up there at the appointed time and found both his bosses at the same table, looking like they were talking about work. Tana Cortes and David Alano were at the veranda, overlooking the bay. Laptops, phones, and coffee cups crowded a table that should have been for six. He knew David had a speech at the hotel first thing that morning and the guy was in a suit sans coat, but Tana was in jeans and a casual top.

They most likely spent the night there, at the hotel.

See, this wasn't so unusual, back when they were on the campaign. Tana and David were earliest at every meeting, last to leave too. Rightly or wrongly, it was a common lunchtime topic whether Tana and David were together, if they lingered post-work because they had other plans, or if they were early because they actually had been together the night before. At the time Ben was in his twenties, and to him

Tana and David were *old* and staff shouldn't be gossiping about what their elders did in their bedrooms. Now that Ben was properly in his thirties, he realized they were just like him—not that old, completely capable of deciding to hop into bed with someone he spent the best or worst day with.

During the campaign, Ben did watch for any signs that this would make things implode within the team, but they never did. Tana's comms and strategy were solid, she disagreed with David as often as anyone else did. The trouble was often from the asshole who eventually got the job everyone felt Tana deserved.

"Ben." David saw him first. He stood up and they did a handshake that became a hug. He had never hugged his boss before, not even when they won the election. This was...well, he was fine with it. He peered over David's shoulder and saw Tana smirking in her seat.

"Morning, Ben," she said. "We'll work from here today, if you don't mind. We haven't completely worked out all the details of the transition."

After letting him go, David motioned for him to pull up a chair. "But I've asked them to start the paperwork on your return to the office."

"Negotiate for no break in years of service," Tana told Ben. "Don't sign anything without checking that part."

"He's a lawyer, Tana. He knows how to check his own employment contract."

"Just want him to know someone has his back, David. Because you didn't."

Ben wasn't sure he wanted to be in this conversation, but it was several months coming. The day he "quit" was the last time he and David even spoke; that week his work phone was disconnected, and the newest of Elmo's assistants had been the only person to get in touch about any job-related loose ends.

"I handled that badly, Ben," David started.

"The worst," Tana said.

"—but it took me a while to figure out how to do this. I apologize for how long it took, Ben, and that it wasn't soon enough, and that it happened the way it did."

"Why *did* it happen the way it did?" Might as well ask it, now that it looked like things were going his way. "Was there a deal with Buena I didn't know about? Or shouldn't have known about?"

"No, nothing like that. I really did think you didn't want to do this anymore."

"Why would you think that?"

"You and Elmo were arguing a lot."

"Because he's an asshole and he argues with everyone."

"Ben, I'm not...I made a bad call, and I'm going to make it up to you, but I'm not as dense as you think. You weren't fine for months. I'm not sure what you're going through, but when the suggestion came up that someone leaving the staff would be the best response, and you sent an email saying it could be you..."

"I sent that email at two a.m. and I was tired and we should have at least talked about it." Ben couldn't believe he was pulling an "I was tired" defense, but it was what it was. "We were all burned out. I shouldn't have found out about my firing on fucking Twitter."

"All of it was handled badly," Tana said, her tone stern. "That entire conversation on attacking Buena should not have happened at all, but it did, and your little boys club couldn't fix what you had broken. It didn't even *work*. You're still so fucked."

Ben was glad she said it, because he wasn't going to.

While scraping the shreds of his dignity he saw the aftermath of his firing, how it never mended things with Senator Buena, how their respective offices continued to butt heads on things they theoretically agreed on. It was giving him flashbacks from the worst of the campaign, but yes under Elmo it was happening almost on a daily basis, and with no end in sight.

So...yes he did look tired in the weeks and months before his firing. He *was* fighting with the staff a lot. Elmo did start to staff the place with people who agreed with him and his politics, and it was wearing out Ben even when Elmo wasn't around.

"I didn't want to quit," Ben insisted.

"Obviously I should have talked to you," David replied. "But I knew that Tana set up her own company and I thought you were quitting to join her. And then you did."

"Hello, don't make me an excuse for anything," Tana said. "I reached out to him when I did because the press on Ben seemed the opposite of everything he is." She cleared her throat and might have kicked David under the table.

"The adjustment's been difficult," David said to Ben, as if on cue. "As a leader, I let some things slide. Understand that it's an honor, to have you back with us. I know you work hard and you work well, and it's not going to be fun—it'll be more difficult from here on out. Tana's made a huge sacrifice to come back to the office, and I know we need to make it right for you as well. But if you're willing to stay, I'd rather continue this with people like you with me."

Ben stole a glance at Tana, and she was typing something on her laptop. He wasn't entirely sure why she agreed to come back either, but when she asked for his help and gave him a job, it was better than moping and being unemployed. He wasn't sure if he should be exploring other things. He wasn't sure if it was the best thing to go back into that circle of hell.

"If you decide to come back," David continued, "you get to keep telling me what you think I should hear. You get to keep me in check. Tana has the same mandate. We should do this for each other."

"No one believes we can actually do anything," Ben said. "I don't know if you're aware. You don't know how many people told me they were happy I was out of politics."

Tana's mouth pulled into a thin line. "Same."

David leaned forward, almost placing himself between them. "Then make it count for you. We're still in a position to get more done on a larger scale, and that's a privilege. Use it."

It sounded like a challenge, to Ben. It sounded like backbone.

Ben had a lot of time to do a lot of thinking, but it was hard to be all decisive about it when he didn't actually have the choice in front of him. Now he did.

True, the job was difficult. True, he was at risk of being burned out. Elmo might not be around anymore, but the very nature of their work meant dealing with people like him, all the time. He focused on this moment, on clearing his work record and getting his job back...but did he have to? Was this what he wanted his life to be?

What kind of monster did he have to be to go back in there?

Because it would never end.

What kind of day do you want this to be? he asked himself.

23

T*hree months later*

DEAR MR. CACHO:

GOOD DAY! My name is Louise Lazaro, third year marketing major at ABLU, Taguig campus. Our home department is hosting its annual career month, and on behalf of the department I wish to invite you to be the main speaker on our second week. If you confirm participation, you will be speaking to about three hundred business management majors and your session will be one hour and thirty minutes long. One of our instructors, Ms. Llamas, recommended you and said your background in law, advocacy work, speech-writing, and politics will be interesting for the students.

We hope you can confirm and we look forward to meeting you. My contact info is included below.

Louise Lazaro

3BM/En

Two weeks later

THE YOUNG MAN hosting the Q&A session after his speech was wearing a suit, and Ben thought that was precious. The young lady was in a pantsuit as well. Both of them in college, in their late teens or early twenties, but dressed in a way that made them look "serious," like adults. Precious, because Ben showed up in blue jeans and a shirt that said *Make Good Days* under a black blazer. Not the same one that he wore when he saw Naya; he actually had several made. To everyone else it was a black shirt, or a blue shirt, or a gray shirt, but he knew that it carried a pep talk to himself, and that was helpful.

Anyway. If the students thought suits made you an adult, eventually they'd learn that it wasn't a uniform, and power could be drawn from something entirely...casual. But he wasn't going to say that just yet, because it was cute. He had finished his speech at the podium, and now he was sitting on a chair on stage, facing the young man and young woman, both of them also on chairs, holding microphones and index cards.

"...consider practicing law?" The young woman's name tag said Louise, and she was asking him this question.

"I don't think so," Ben answered. "I was fortunate to have done well in law school, but it wasn't for me."

"Do you regret going through it? Because that's years of your life too."

"I try not to regret things," he said. Softer than his answer on job interviews, for sure, but he didn't want to give anyone in the auditorium the wrong impression. "What happened is I...didn't question it. It was my path, and when the financial and health difficulties hit my family, I had to make the decision, and I decided to stay on. I'm not practicing now but being there led me to the most fulfilling career I've ever had. I can't say I was wrong to have stayed."

"So I think I'm not alone in being a little surprised by how you talk about your work," the young man, name tag Pau, said. "It always seemed to me that politics is a dirty job that only people with the worst intentions try to do."

"I'm not here to change that," Ben said. "A survival tip: when you feel that way about someone you work with, in government or any career, don't let your guard down. A lot about this that you learn on the job is figuring out what people *want*. Sometimes because you need to know it so you can write the things that they'll understand; sometimes it's so you know the words to use to reach them. Sometimes when people gain this insight, they use that influence for themselves, or for something that doesn't help people. Yes we have to guard against that, all the time. So yeah, if I came up here and made you think politics is nice and fun because I said the right things, don't completely let go of your gut instinct."

"So you're saying we shouldn't believe what you say?" said Louise.

Ben shrugged, smiling. "Some people like saying, 'I

know exactly what's good for you, trust me.' I won't be saying that. Even on your career day."

"Are you rare?" Pau asked.

"What?"

"We don't think of someone like you, when we think of people who have your job. Are we wrong? Are you actually one of a kind?"

Ben frowned. "I'm...I'm not rare. I'm not the best there is. Someone in this room could do a better job, eventually, because I've made mistakes that you can avoid I'm sure."

"What advice do you have for someone who now wants to be like you, after hearing you speak here today?"

"Ha. Surround yourself with people you admire, who do good things." Ben looked out into the auditorium, to the escalating rows of students, hundreds of them, and remembered something. "That's bullshit advice by the way and it sounds easy when you're here in school, because everyone's got a lot of energy. Out there, in any career, you'll be with people who are jaded and tired and might resent your energy. Or you'll be in a place where you can't choose who you're with, it's just not possible. If that's the case...hang on to *this*. What you feel now. Who you know here. Or go on breaks and meet people who can bring that into your life again."

"Do you think there are people who can do this, and people who can't?" Pau asked.

"I don't know how to answer that," Ben said. "I said earlier, I didn't plan to be a speechwriter. Didn't know if my candidate would win the senate seat because there are so few of them. There's a lot of uncertainty in my job, and I'm sure for other people too. Sometimes we don't have the privilege of choosing to live our dreams. I work with people who are not at all passionate about this, and that's okay. Find your motivation somewhere, anywhere."

"I have one last question," Louise said, shuffling her cards. "Tell us what your best day on the job was like."

He laughed. "There was this one day...I got fired. Spent a whole day doing other things, with other people. Best day ever."

"That's not a day on the job!"

"My career is all my jobs, all the decisions I made," Ben said. "That day is part of it. I walked into a van by mistake, and it was the best decision ever."

∼

WHERE WAS NAYA?

That had been on Ben's mind all day, plus two weeks. When he got the email invitation to speak he had said yes, and then cancelled a meeting with his new team of writers too so his sked would be clear that day. He hadn't heard from Naya at all since she walked out of his apartment, and then this? He didn't know she had started teaching, but it made sense.

The next day, he left a message on her tour page, thanking her for the recommendation.

He didn't get a response.

But the email thread with Louise and Pau was active, so he'd be speaking at their school event whether Naya ignored him or not. Ben asked for what exactly they needed him to say, and was able to tease out from them that this was a marketing exercise as well. So Ben wrote a version of his usual "how I got my job" talk but making sure to mention how marketing and branding concepts were helping him.

He might have asked for a Q&A forum after his talk, in

case their teacher would like to participate. Louise said no worries, they had already drafted questions, and she and Pau would be hosting. Ms. Llamas had wanted them to handle the event from start to finish.

Will she even be there? He wanted to ask, but didn't, because seeing her was not the point. It wasn't why he said yes. He said he'd give the talk because he wanted the kids to learn something...okay so it was forty-five percent why he said yes.

In any case he didn't see her at all in the auditorium, and at the end of it had to take several zillion photos with many students, and didn't see her then either.

Not the point, he reminded himself.

She would get in touch, if she was ready to see him. She knew where he lived. He spent almost half the year getting his life back on track, and he was getting antsy about three months? Not fair.

He missed her, but yeah.

"Hi," said the student who was shaking his hand after taking a photo with him, "you seem nice but you just reminded all of us not to trust you."

Ben shook himself slightly, forced himself to focus on right now. "It's good to question the way things are, is what I say. Might lead to more reasons to trust, anyway."

"Or we could end up like you."

Ben put a hand to his heart. The students surrounding him giggled. "I'm not sure if that's a compliment or not."

He didn't tell them the story of the wall of monsters, how he and Naya still identified with those grotesque creatures, even if they could be considered "good guys." Maybe that was too cynical to share. If only he could have talked to Naya about it.

Or talk about it with her now.

"So, where's Ms. Llamas?" Ben asked, as the last of the students filed out of the auditorium. "I'd like to see her before I head out."

"She's coming," Louise said. "She just texted me."

Maybe it was better this way, that she hadn't watched him speak, that he didn't see her, that he could contain his inevitable response to her or at least have it be witnessed by only a few people. Maybe this was—

"Ben!"

It was a familiar voice; just not the one he was expecting.

Benjamin Cacho

So I'm here, sitting on your chair. At the faculty room. I wanted to ask you what happened, why you're teaching marketing now. But apparently you're not, and instead you're teaching Web Video, and the Ms. Llamas whose students invited me to speak to the business majors was Melly, and not you. It was confusing, but I'm all caught up. I forgot she had the same last name? But then I remembered that I don't know everything about everyone in the world, and I got over it. I asked Melly if I could talk to you, but of course that is entirely up to you, but she said I could sit here in the faculty room and that would be fine, because I spoke in her class today.

How are you, Naya?

See This Manila

No, it was my idea to invite you. She needed a speaker for career day and I thought you'd be great. Were you? I'm pretty sure you were.

I'm fine, Ben. Thanks for asking.

Benjamin **Cacho**
    She replies!
    I think I did okay. I don't know if any of them are going
to follow this career path, but I hope I impressed upon them
the idea that we all have to work hard, and continue to be
compassionate.

See **This Manila**
    Did you tell them that they'll need to choose their
monster?

Benjamin **Cacho**
    I didn't. Damn. I wanted to ask you if I should say that.

See **This Manila**
    Maybe that's too advanced. Or too personal.

Benjamin **Cacho**
    I tried to get in touch with you but you didn't reply.

See **This Manila**
    I'm replying now.

Benjamin **Cacho**

Why aren't you here?

SEE This Manila
Took the class on a little trip. Still on-campus, but not in the building. I won't be going back there. Sorry I missed your talk.

BENJAMIN Cacho
You had to take them out of the building the same day I'd be here?

SEE This Manila
I arranged the speaking gig, Ben. You needed me to cheer you on?

BENJAMIN Cacho
I miss you. That's all.

SEE This Manila
Oh.
We can meet today.
If you have time.

BENJAMIN Cacho
I have nothing but time, Naya. Took a leave and everything.

SEE This Manila

I feel so special. See you at sunset?

BENJAMIN Cacho

Where?

SEE This Manila

The best place to watch it. According to me.

BENJAMIN Cacho

You told me where that was, right?

SEE This Manila

I told you where to find it.

24

Intramuros, 5:20 p.m.

TAKING a leave for the entire work day for a ninety-minute speaking engagement seemed over the top, but soon he was congratulating himself on the foresight. If he hadn't done that, he wouldn't be free to travel across the metro in the afternoon, right in the middle of rush hour. At this time of year, the nights were longer, and the sun set earlier.

He would have missed the best sunset view in the city, according to travel expert Naya Llamas.

It had rained in the afternoon the past two days, but this day was thankfully dry, and the sky was beginning to turn orange-pink behind hovering light gray clouds. Parking was a little bit of a hassle but eventually, hotel security helped him out, alerting him to a free space across the street. He made it to the rooftop restaurant right on time.

Right on time. For what? Sunset was about to begin, but it happened every day.

Ben saw her on the roof deck, holding her phone to take a photo of the view. She looked exactly as she did when they met, like she was dressed for a tour. Ponytail, tee, jeans that looked comfortable. If he didn't clear his throat indiscreetly, she probably wouldn't have turned around.

Which underscored how likely it was that she didn't need him. Wasn't waiting with bated breath for him.

Still, there they were.

If he was seeing her for the first time, on this roof, would he approach her and say hello? Ben didn't do that, on regular days. He was the kind who braced himself for social gatherings, hid in kitchens when it got too overwhelming. If he were on this roof and he saw her, he'd look, and...not do anything. And that would be his mistake. If Naya had issues about his travel persona versus his real one, then too bad—that "real guy," he no longer existed. Ben looked and felt exactly the same, but he knew he was different. Like someone told him to look in another direction—and there it was, a stunning sunset, impossible to look away from and forever in his memory. He couldn't explain it. It had a lot to do with her, and he wanted her to know that. He wanted to introduce her to the person she helped create.

Naya smiled, then shook her head a little. "You wear the same thing every time I see you."

It wasn't even intentional. He did wear this, and variations of this, every day. If he saw her tomorrow, she'd see him in pretty much the same outfit. She didn't realize how much she'd already seen, how much of him only she knew.

Or maybe she did.

"You too," he said. "Hi, Naya Llamas. I'm Benjamin

Cacho. Legal age. Joining you on this roof deck of my own free will..."

She blinked. "We don't have to do this."

"...joining you wherever you want to take me, out of my own free will..."

"*Ben.* You sound like you're saying vows. Stop being weird."

"—let me finish or it won't be binding—I promise you if any pain befalls me on this journey, it will be entirely my fault. There, you will not be liable. Please take me with you."

"Oh my God." She looked away, toward the sky changing color, and then faced him again. "You're kind of dramatic."

"I think it's a good idea. In case you're not sure if I know what I'm signing up for."

"That's not binding."

"You have my word. I like giving my words value."

~

Dear God, why does he sound like he's reading a contract, and why is it still kind of hot?

When did she become into this? Into guys who wore practically one kind of outfit. Who worked in government. Who lived close enough to have a real relationship with. Naya thought about it, and came to the following conclusions: the outfit suited him, so why mess with it; yes, he worked for a senator and she'd call him out on shit if she needed to; proximity was not a bad thing. That last one was what she'd mulled over the longest. She was an adult, damn it. Naya wanted to think that if she wanted to end a dry spell she could do so in a responsible manner with another consenting adult, and not have to slink into a relationship to do it.

But here they were.

"I should tell you that I've never really been in a relationship before," Naya said.

His brow quirked. "That's what this is?"

"Isn't it?"

"Fair enough. Yes, that's what this should be, I think."

"I *have never* been in one. Like, with no pre-determined ending. And with the other party pretty much in the next neighborhood. Have you?"

"No relationship experience either," he admitted. "But it was because of law school, then work. Always work."

Oh wow. She was looking at him but also looking past him, at the best sunset view in the city. In her heart of hearts, the best in the world. He saw that her attention was divided and he looked outward too, toward a Manila skyline that was layered, complicated.

"Wow," he said. "It's...different here."

"Different how?"

"Sunset by the bay is beautiful. It's seeing the sun dip into the water. It's always awesome. But this..."

This was the same sky, colored by fire, showing a city that was old, and new, and rebuilt, and built over. It was a Manila that was shiny tall buildings, and dilapidated houses, and within quick minutes it would plunge into darkness, and be lit instead by electric stars.

"It's everything," Naya said. "I'm not afraid of flaws."

"I love that about you. Your passion for things—I might have caught it."

"You already had it."

"Not the way you do."

"If we're going to do this, if we're going to be in a relationship...I think we should figure out how to be with each other on normal days. Like, when things aren't completely falling apart for either of us."

"That'll be easy."

"You're such an optimist."

"What would a normal day look like, anyway?"

Okay, so even Naya had to pause. "I teach three times a week now. And schedule tours one day a week, if I can fill it up."

Ben shrugged. "I'm deputy communications director now, so I have staff. Work's still work, but I can take days off like this when I have to."

"Wednesday nights are dinners out with Melly. No boys allowed."

"I'm sure I'll be able to find something to do."

"I like good food and all but when it's just me, I'll probably be having instant ramen."

Ben flinched. "Okay, that we can work on. Or I can make you my emergency sandwiches."

"Whole wheat bread."

"Okay."

"Okay."

They both stepped closer to each other, and Naya's mind kind of blanked. She felt his hand grab hers, and then he was close enough to kiss.

"Is that all?" Ben asked, as if surprised. "Did we cover all the important stuff?"

Yes—no—"Of course not," Naya said. "But we'll make it work."

"One day at a time."

"Yes."

"So we start today. What kind of day do you want it to be?"

It *was* a good day. She taught her two classes, and it was

easy for her to get into that groove. Naya was sharing what she knew, and it was something the school found important. She received some nice messages from this guy. She headed over to this hotel to prepare for a future tour.

It was a regular day.

She raised her hand, touched his mouth with her fingers. Then kissed him. This was *fine*. It was wonderful. It was a kiss that he wanted, and gave back. It fit into her good, regular day.

Their days would be like this now. Not bad at all.

EPILOGUE

O*ne month later*

SATURDAYS WERE NOW the best days.

Reclaim your weekends was advice from Naya that was easy to take, because she also provided the best reason to do it. He did work on weekends usually, but there was a lot to do and no good reason to refuse any of it.

The thing David said about him being burned out— okay, made sense.

Now Saturdays were the best. He still worked late hours on most days but the transition to Tana taking over as chief of staff came with a more forgiving approach to no-work weekends. He didn't want to completely shut off so he developed an alert system with his new team, and so far, four weeks already, nothing had needed escalation.

So, four weeks now, he'd been able to spend Saturday waking up beside her.

And get decent hours of sleep at the same time. Best life.

That day, however, he woke up with a seed of dread in his gut, and he realized what it was.

"Ah shit," Ben said, pushing his face into her neck, a thing he liked to do now, but this time partly to hide from what he knew was going to happen.

"I'm going with you," Naya said, apparently already awake. "It won't be as bad as it usually is."

"Do you promise."

"I thought you said things were better when we did it together, Ben."

"I meant sex. And that one time you went to the bank with me."

"Sexy banking."

"Sexy waiting in line for things."

"You know what this is, right? The whole newness of it. You love everything."

"I didn't love the ferry ride." Ben recently had the so-called pleasure of riding the Pasig River Ferry, thanks to Naya. He didn't get sick on the boat, didn't fall into the water, but he wasn't swearing off land transport anytime soon.

"Exactly. You won't love everything, even if we're doing it together. And maybe that's okay."

He knew that, of course. But maybe for the first time in his life he could let go a little, and let someone in, and trust someone when she said the boat ride on unclean water wouldn't kill him.

It didn't kill him. He didn't find it as fascinating as she did, but it didn't kill him.

Relationships were about compromise, apparently.

"You know what, you don't have to go to this party," she said.

"I wish."

"You can do whatever you want."

"It's Esteban's chief of staff."

She laughed, still a lovely sound even when slightly mocking his drama. "I don't even know what that means."

"It means I should be there, and I already said I'd go."

"Then we'll go. I love that restaurant. We go for the food, every time."

She was still in the middle of that sentence when the reflex kicked in, which was great because he had been training himself not to forget it.

You don't get to complain, because this is another day with her.

"Fine, fine," Ben said, closing his eyes, pressing his face more into her neck, falling into peppermint-scented comfort. "I won't argue."

"It's okay to argue."

"Oh I know how you get when you're all fired up, lady. I think I'll save my energy for that party I don't like."

"I don't think so."

He heard this, not seeing her face because of how they were spooning, but he could imagine her smile, the look of mischief in her eye.

"I think," she said. "You should spend *all* your energy now on something else. Then sleep and recharge for later."

He didn't see her face but he felt her push back against him, making her intentions very clear.

∼

SHE SAID she knew where they were going, and of course he was going to trust her.

Yes, he still hated the parties. Years on the job, and after fighting to get it back—his "reward" was attending someone's chief of staff's birthday at this French restaurant.

A server had approached him and asked if he wanted *vins rouges*. Ben had blinked. He knew what was being asked, but he just stood there, not choosing.

"Red or white?" As promised, Naya had stayed by his side the entire time. Sure it had been barely an hour since they arrived, but he'd been distracted by the whispered explaining of who this person was and why they had to say hello. She seemed unfazed by the VIPs in attendance, even when people reacted to her being introduced as his girlfriend.

Well, that was what she was. Ben admired her poise.

"We should go to France," he'd said. "We should go everywhere. We shouldn't be staying too long in places like this."

She'd smiled at the server and shrugged. "Nothing for us right now, thank you. Ben, let's go this way."

They weaved through the important people, then made it to a side door, that led them out into an empty hall. Marble floor, high ceiling, illuminated by a token lamp by the door. But they weren't done walking. He followed her out a smaller door, down a lit hallway, and up a flight of stairs in what seemed to be another building. A hallway of lockers on one side, and closed doors on the other. She peeked through the glass insert of one door, then he was being pulled inside.

When she flipped a switch and light flooded the room, he saw they were in...a kitchen? An empty kitchen. But with rows of long tables, set up like a classroom.

"It's a kitchen lab," Naya whispered. She smiled. "There's a culinary school literally connected to the restaurant. I've been to a cookie-making class here. Thought it might relax you."

He was about to object to that, but the point was he was away from the party, and they probably would have been kicked out from the actual kitchen. It was a good time to think about that, why he wanted to retreat when he was at events like this one. Hiding in the kitchen—or anywhere—didn't help him relax. They helped him pass the time until it was fine to leave.

Maybe he was extra nervous, because this was the first event since he got back to work, and certain people he never cared for would be around. Maybe it had to do with how he'd introduced Naya to David and Tana, and him suddenly thinking it was like she'd met his parents.

Workplace parents, in a way, because his mom and dad would never get to meet her.

It was a lot to unpack.

Still, he was with her, and it was better than all the days without her.

He knew this.

They could kiss in here, couldn't they? Not that it mattered to him because he just did, right there, and then she pushed him against the wall and kissed him back. Campus security could reprimand them later, if they wanted to at all.

"Why do you know all the best places?" he asked, between kisses.

"Listen to yourself," she said. "This is just a classroom. You make it sound like it's everything."

"You're everything. You know that, don't you?"

Her breath, and the words she tried to form, tickled his lips. "We make good days."

"Do I? For you?"

"Yes, you do."

That was everything to him, as well.

The End

AUTHOR'S NOTE

My next contemporary romance series was supposed to have been set in the world of politics. I had outlined three books, started my research, named the characters. That was years ago, and frankly my head is in another place regarding elected officials. My heart too—so those books won't be written anymore.

Then the idea for this book came and I was able to "save" three characters from that shelved series, and place them here. It's a different world, so I changed them accordingly. While I do like to challenge myself when writing characters, and I've taken on the "unlikeable" in the past, I decided not to do so here. I won't make this a space where truly terrible people are somehow redeemed. Ben, David, and Tana are good people; always have been, always will be. I didn't use any of the real-world research here too, so if anything resembles real life, it's unintentional.

That said, the tour of Manila *can* be recreated and made better even. If you're ever in town, let's eat somewhere.

Thank you to this book's team: Layla, Veronica, Tania, Pach, Alex, Bibo, Graie, Janus, R, S, and I.

ABOUT THE AUTHOR

Mina V. Esguerra writes contemporary romance, young adult, and new adult novellas. Visit her website minavesguerra.com for more about her books, talks, and events.

When not writing romance, she is president of communications firm Bronze Age Media, a development communication consultant, and a publisher. She created the workshop series "Author at Once" for writers and publishers, and #romanceclass for aspiring romance writers. Her young adult/fantasy trilogy Interim Goddess of Love is a college love story featuring gods from Philippine mythology. Her contemporary romance novellas won the Filipino Readers' Choice awards for Chick Lit in 2012 (Fairy Tale Fail) and 2013 (That Kind of Guy).

She has a bachelor's degree in Communication and a master's degree in Development Communication.

Six 32 Central series: What Kind of Day

Chic Manila series: My Imaginary Ex | Fairy Tale Fail | No Strings Attached | Love Your Frenemies | That Kind of Guy | Welcome to Envy Park | Wedding Night Stand (short story) | What You Wanted | Iris After the Incident | Better At Weddings Than You

Addison Hill series: Falling Hard | Fallen Again | Learning to Fall

Breathe Rockstar Romance series: Playing Autumn | Tempting Victoria | Kissing Day (short story)

Scambitious series: Young and Scambitious | Properly Scandalous | Shiny and Shameless | Greedy and Gullible

Interim Goddess of Love series: Interim Goddess of Love | Queen of the Clueless | Icon of the Indecisive | Gifted Little Creatures (short story) | Freshman Girl and Junior Guy (short story)

The Future Chosen

Anthology contributions: Say That Things Change (New Adult Quick Reads 1) | Kids These Days: Stories from Luna East Arts Academy Volume 1 | Sola Musica: Love Notes from a Festival | Make My Wish Come True | Summer Feels

Contact Mina

minavesguerra.com
minavesguerra@gmail.com

BOOKS BY FILIPINO AUTHORS
#ROMANCECLASS

romanceclass

Visit romanceclassbooks.com to read more
romance/contemporary/YA by Filipino authors.

CPSIA information can be obtained
at www.ICGtesting.com
Printed in the USA
LVHW04s1845090718
583162LV00003B/630/P

9 781719 234740